# LAST STAND AT ANVIL PASS

**Merle Constiner** was born in Monroe, Ohio. Other than the years he spent at Vanderbilt University, earning a Master's degree in Journalism, he lived his whole life in Monroe. It wasn't until the 1940s that he began publishing detective fiction extensively in pulp magazines like *Black Mask* and *Dime Detective Magazine*. In the 1950s he began contributing fiction to such slick magazines as *The Saturday Evening Post* and *The American Magazine*. It was first at the end of the decade that he published two original paperback Westerns, *Last Stand at Anvil Pass* (Fawcett, 1957) and *The Fourth Gunman* (Ace, 1958). Yet it wasn't until the 1960s, beginning with *Short-Trigger Man* (Ace, 1964), that Constiner came to specialize in Western fiction, producing a body of work that not only established his reputation but continues to retain its popularity with readers. He wrote in a simple, straightforward manner and populated his stories with unusual and memorable characters. *Death Waits at Dakins Station* (Ace, 1970) is both characteristic and typical of Constiner at his best, the story of an unemployed cowpuncher who is hired to take a message to Dakins Station and as a result finds himself in a complex intrigue. The ironic humor with which the story is told in this and his other books comprises the charm of his style. Constiner always attends to historical detail, geographic as well as social, and however conventional a situation may seem at first, his protagonists do not react quite like any others in Western fiction, an attribute of his Western stories that never allows them to lose their attraction and interest.

# LAST STAND AT
# ANVIL PASS

## Merle Constiner

**GUNSMOKE**

First published in the US by Crest Books

This hardback edition 2013
by AudioGO Ltd
by arrangement with
Golden West Literary Agency

ISBN 978 1 471 32055 2

**British Library Cataloguing in Publication Data available.**

Printed and bound in Great Britain by
MPG Books Group Limited

# 1

DRESSING in his hotel room for his weekly Tuesday-morning visit with Dove, John Sennett's thoughts were on another matter. Mentally he made a listing. *Dead*: *Browne, Knutson, Wilkins, and Mrs. Wilkins. Homes and barns burned*: *four. Ranchers driven from the county*: *three.* They'd told him that if a range war broke he would be one of the first to be caught in the whirlwind; actually, it had passed him by. He looked at his big silver watch, which was engraved with deer and hounds. Three minutes to ten. Absently, he put on his gunbelt and walked to the window.

His Colt was shiny and unused, its holster and belt stiff and squeaky. To Sennett it was simply an article of merchandise from his store and he was scarcely aware that he wore it. He had another in his trunk, a weapon he had used as deputy to his father in the wild Tombigbee Swamp of Alabama before he had come West, but it was so battle-scarred and finger-worn that he winced from flaunting it.

Below the window lay Main Street, scorching in the

sun and brassy with dust. This little town of Napier had treated him well. In three years, by fatigue and foresight, he had acquired this building which was the hotel, a third of the stageline, and the town's largest general store. He owned a ranch, too, a tiny spread out at the edge of the valley. Around this ranch now flamed the range war.

His garish gunbelt creaking, he left the room, descended the stairs to the lobby, and emerged on the boardwalk. Todd Hatty was sitting on his heels in a patch of violet shade by the doorway. He rose slowly. Sennett knew that now, at last, the danger was on him.

The Hatty outfit was behind the big trouble.

Formally, they stared at each other, Sennett rawly alert, Todd lazy in the belief that he was inspiring fear. He was Old Man Hatty's son, about Sennett's age, short, and muscled like a blacksmith's striker. Pink stubble sparkled on his cheeks and his eye sockets were bloated and red. He gave off a musky animal odor. Woodenly, he said, "My father wants to see you. He's around at your store."

Sennett nodded and started down the walk, the cumbersome holster at his thigh squeaking. Todd swung in beside him and said drolly, "Gun and all."

Walking stiffly, keeping his eyes straight ahead, Sennett considered events. The thing had burst into thunder a month ago, though the storm had been gathering for a year. A good half of the valley, the northern half, was Hatty range, extensive but mediocre. The Hattys had long coveted the better grass of the small ranchers to the south and were now trying to expand. They struck with violence and terror, but they made a solemn show of legality.

A particular thing had sparked them into action. The valley was egg-shaped, closed in by rugged uplands, and had but two exits. The northern pass, which was on Hatty land, was a fine broad egress that had once been a military road. The southern exit, hardly more than a brushy defile between two peaks known as Big and Little Anvil, was on Sennett's small ranch. Until recently, it had been considered useless, worthless. Now, beyond this pass, surveyors were scouting a railroad. The Hattys moved. They wanted the southern valley and Sennett's pass.

The first signs were the horsemen. Riders strange to

6

Napier drifted into town on Hatty mounts. Out in the county, disaster struck south valley ranchers. Knutson had been found riddled in his barn. Wilkins and Mrs. Wilkins had been ambushed by "outlaws." In town, at the Napier Livery Stable, Sawyer Browne had been slain openly.

But Sennett himself, and his Anvil Pass, had seemingly been ignored.

Now, as Todd Hatty walked beside him, Sennett once more saw the evil thing as it had unfolded. They passed down Main Street and turned into Congress Street.

Halfway along Congress Street was Sennett's store, serving most of the county. An enormous building, stark under a thin coat of yellow paint, it had mushroomed in importance until it soon would be having its own subsidiary bank. Behind the store was Sennett's big public hitching lot, and the loading platform for freight wagons.

Todd and Sennett passed down an alley at the side of the store and came in from the rear. They climbed timber steps to the platform, walked along it, and entered a door and a passage.

Here were the smells of Sennett's stockrooms, the smells which gave him such a feeling of reality and life: dried apples, tar, bolt cloth, rope. He was icy with anger at the outrage which was searing the county, and at the man who walked beside him, but no sign of it showed on his tired face. At a second door, Sennett's office, Todd dropped to his heels in the hallway. Resting his back against the wall, he watched Sennett enter, alone.

Breathing slowly, in imprisoned indignation, Sennett crossed the threshold.

Three people were in the room. Old Man Hatty, in sweaty black broadcloth and lumpy boots, lolled in Sennett's chair. He was bent, knotty, and withered. Once his name had been the glory and pride of the county, but those days were long gone. Greed and venom and arrogance glazed his eyes. By his shoulder stood Ellen Browne, and on a nail keg in the corner sat Sheriff Lytle. Old Man Hatty said curtly, "Well, it took you long enough."

Sennett looked at the girl, keeping the confusion out of his eyes. She was tall, yellow-haired, and dressed in crisp black, in mourning for her father, -just buried.

He scarcely knew her, but he had known her father well. Sawyer Browne, the largest owner in the south valley,

7

had been Hatty's most outspoken opposition. He had been in the process of organizing his neighbors, of forming a South Valley Association, when a Hatty rider had goaded him and then slain him. Sennett was shocked to see her consorting with her father's enemy.

Of course there was more to it than that, if you could believe rumor. Rumor had it that there had long been friction—some said outright bad feeling—between Ellen and her father.

But bad feeling or no, she was in mighty bad company and, in Sennett's opinion, there was no excuse for it.

He gave her a quick second look, saw that her eyes were fastened on him, coldly, impersonally, then turned his attention to the others.

Sheriff Lytle cleared his throat. "Mr. Sennett," he said importantly, "you'll be glad to hear all this ruckus is over—thanks to the wisdom of Mr. Hatty."

Sennett waited in silence. He felt unfriendliness about him, in varying degrees. With Old Man Hatty it was open contempt, with the sheriff it was caution. With Ellen Browne it was simply a barrier.

He was a townsman and not a countyman. He was a merchant and not, in their eyes, a genuine cattleman. And most grievous from their viewpoint was the fact that he lived in his hotel in Napier while someone else managed the ranch he owned.

"When you come right down to it," said Old Man Hatty, "all this fuss and feathers ain't nothing but a bunch of high-spirited cowhands from different spreads finding out one another's weight. That's natural in young fellows, shooting off pistols and such, but it can get out of control. Like Sheriff Lytle says, I've figured out a way to put a stop to it. I'm taking Miss Browne and her South Association into my North Association, so we'll be one big family."

"I didn't know you had a North Association," said Sennett.

"Well, you know it now."

"We want you to join us," said Ellen Browne. "It's the only thing."

Sheriff Lytle nodded in vigorous agreement.

"It's entirely up to him," said Old Man Hatty harshly. "I want him to get that straight. I don't care one way or the other."

"What do I put in?" asked Sennett affably.

"Nothing," said Old Man Hatty.

8

Just my prestige and my self respect and Anvil Pass, thought Sennett.

"You put in nothing but your good will," said Hatty. "Then sit back and collect the benefits."

Ellen said quietly, "I didn't expect a remark like that, Mr. Sennett, from a gentleman of your reputation. Here we are dealing with human lives and you say, 'What do I put in.'"

Old Man Hatty gave a brittle laugh. "His good reputation is for making money, Ellen." He screwed up his face and lowered his head. "You know what? I almost called you daughter."

Ellen stared at him. "Daughter?"

Somehow the Old Man managed to look heart-broken and embarrassed. The pretense was so obvious that Sennett could hardly stomach it.

"Yes, daughter," mumbled Old Man Hatty. "It's been coming over me for years now. You know I had a little girl that died a long time ago. She'd be about your age now. She had the same pretty yellow hair you got, and the same unselfish heart."

"That's right," said Sheriff Lytle, touched.

"I remember her," said Ellen softly. "She was lovely."

I don't remember her, Sennett thought. But I've heard about her. I heard she died of downright neglect.

"I'm a little busy this morning," Sennett said patiently. "I wonder if we could stick to the point?"

Old Man Hatty's little eyes revolved slowly, and lighted on him.

"They's just one thing more. When you come into our group you get rid of Jim Trego, of course. He's always been a troublemaker to this valley."

Now, curiously, Sennett gazed at Ellen Browne. His foreman, Trego, had been her father's closest friend, and Trego had criticized the Hattys garrulously, at every opportunity. He was one of the county's true old-timers, and a fine foreman.

Beneath Sennett's inquiring glance, Ellen Browne said, "Mr. Hatty's right. Trego will have to leave the county. He's incorrigible."

"I see," said Sennett.

"Well, I'm busy this morning, too," said Old Man Hatty. "Make up your mind. What about it?"

Sennett said, "No."

"How's that again?"

"I said no. I'm not interested."

Hatty's bloodless lips curled in rage. Sheriff Lytle lumbered to his feet, nervous and confused.

A numbness seemed to come over them, and in that silence Sennett left the room.

In the hall, Todd asked, "Everything fixed up?" and Sennett said, "Yes, indeed." He left the building, crossed the lot, and walked east on Plum Street, heading for Dove's.

He was annoyed that Hatty and Ellen and Sheriff Lytle could so misjudge him, that he could move among them for three years and they should know him no better.

As he walked, smelling horse dung baking to chaff in the road, hearing cicadas screaming and vibrating in the dusty heat, memories of his boyhood somehow came back to him. Memories of the wild swamp. For a hundred years the great Tombigbee Swamp of southern Alabama, midway between its sisters, the secret bayous of Louisiana and the felon sanctuaries of Florida, had been a way station for the most vicious criminals.

Motherless, he had been raised by his sheriff father at the swamp's edge. Day and night, it seemed to him, his father had tutored him. That had been his boyhood as he remembered it, ceaselessly learning things: Greek and marksmanship and arithmetic, home remedies for bleeding wounds, blue vitriol or oak fungus. At the age of seventeen he had learned enough to become a deputy to his father.

Three years ago, when his father had died, he had felt suddenly hemmed in, and had come West. He had visited Napier, and had remained.

He had found the town flourishing, bursting its seams, yet constricted by miserly, backward business concepts. Its two general stores were small and dirty, frugally stocked, slovenly run. It had but one hotel, and here the same careless insufficiencies prevailed. So much money was coming in over counters that the customer was improperly and inadequately accommodated. Calmly, Sennett had decided to take a chance. He had bought a store, and had gambled his entire capital on good stock for its shelves. His success was so great that in a year he had moved to larger quarters. That was the beginning. Later, he had acquired the hotel.

It was in these early days that he had met Dove Stafford.

Now, thinking of his set-to with Hatty, he decided not to distress her with it.

The Stafford house, at the end of Plum Street, was big and tan, with chocolate-brown shutters. Its yard was grassless and eroded, but the place was Napier's most pretentious. Years ago Sennett had proposed to Dove, and she had accepted him, but nothing seemed to come of it. At first he had fought this vague delay; eventually he had adjusted himself to it.

At first she had given him the idea, indirectly, that it was her mother who had blocked the immediacy of the wedding—not that he wasn't highly eligible to her mother, she hastily explained. Mothers were just that way, reluctant to lose their only daughters. As time went on, and he pressed her, she laid the blame whimsically upon her father. Fathers were that way about their daughters; maybe a little jealous. Don't rush, be patient, things would work out in time. The Staffords, she explained, had always believed in long engagements. What could she and Sennett do? Only be patient and wait, she declared.

For a long time Sennett had believed these things, and had been fooled. Gradually, however, he formed his own opinion. It was Dove herself who was delaying.

She was just a child, he decided. A child, bewildered and a little frightened, perhaps, who wavered at the very brink of marriage. This put a new light on the matter. He could certainly be patient with Dove, always guiding her, always encouraging her—for she was to be his life-long wife.

At any moment, he told himself, she would say yes. Any day now she might set the date.

She was just a child, but only in her indecisions. As a woman she disturbed and attracted him beyond reason, or beyond experience, at times almost unbearably. On many a sultry night, on his little cot in his hotel room, he had awakened, sweaty and tense, with her image in his mind.

Frankly and honestly, he had told her of these terrible moments. She had understood perfectly. She was subject to precisely the same trouble—only much more intolerable, much more wracking. They would have to steel themselves. Life was like that.

Everything was going to work out all right, and soon; she'd guarantee that.

11

Sennett climbed the chocolate-brown steps, and rapped gently.

Dove opened the screen door and he followed her into the cool dark hallway.

She was a small girl, thin and pale, always taut in movement but lazy and deliberate in speech. Sometimes he wondered if it were this strange paradox in her which moved him so provocatively. Now, as she stood before him, she was fragrant with sandalwood and soap. He said, "I can't stay this morning. I just wanted a look at you. I must get out to Anvil."

"Always hustle and bustle," she fretted. Affectionately, she began issuing instructions for his welfare. "Stay out of the heat." And that would be a trick, he thought, amused, with the valley like an oven. "Don't drink at any creek; open water is dangerous this time of the year. Don't dismount at Calico Gulch, it's full of snakes. Don't—"

He kissed her gently, and she responded in that instinctive, eager way he found so shattering.

"How's the garden party coming?" he asked, after a moment.

She flushed with excitement. "Wonderfully."

As he left her and went down the steps, that old feeling of incompleteness came over him once more. It wasn't frustration, he had told himself repeatedly. Frustration would be a shoddy, physical thing. This was much different. He needed her, as she needed him. And they were insufficient without each other.

Returning to Stable Street for his roan, Sennett felt suddenly dog-tired. Strain of overwork, pressure of business, was telling on him, he knew.

Stable Street was a wide, short alley off Main, flanked with ramshackle buildings. Despite its squalor, it was the town's true center of activity, for here were the three livery stables. The largest of these was the Napier Livery; an unofficial club for the county's most important cattlemen. A passage separated it from a feed store on its left, and in this passage, always shady, was a line of chairs and a crude bench, hugging the stable wall. Many important things had occurred here, among them the death of Sawyer Browne. Now, as Sennett turned from the walk into the passageway, he found himself in the midst of a group of men.

In their center stood Holly Fashner, a south valley rancher, talking excitedly. He was a bull of a man, grimy, bespangled with an excess of coin silver trappings. Sennett disliked him, and had been watching him for three years with growing speculation. At the moment, Fashner's fingers were splayed and his mouth was swollen with agitation.

"I'm telling you, gentlemen, it's all over town," he wheezed. "The Browne outfit has throwed in with Hatty and formed one big pack. What are we little folks going to do?"

Before his audience could answer, he raised his voice. "I was a loyal Sawyer Browne man, but I ain't no Ellen Browne man. She's turned against her dead daddy, and she's turned against us. They ain't been enough night riding and bushwhacking so she went to Hatty and tossed in her guns with his to help it along. Gentlemen, we got to take over the South Valley Association before we perish, and I mean here and now."

There was a murmur of confusion, and faltering agreement.

One voice, however, dissented. A soft Alabama drawl, sweet to Sennett's ears, said, "I vote we don't go off half-cocked. I vote we all go home and set a while and study it over."

Sennett gazed at the speaker. Two old men were huddled alone at one end of the bench. They were wizened and wrinkled, with incredibly clear blue eyes. Sennett knew them by hearsay. They were newcomers, their name was Durben, and they lived in poverty in a shack in the foothills. They were brothers. One had a silky mustache, the other a bear-clawed chin. The brother with the mustache was the spokesman.

Fashner said brutally, "When I want your advice, I'll ask for it."

"You just did. You said what we little folks going to do?"

"I was talking to these other men. This here's a pow-wow for south valley ranchers."

"Us Durbens is south valley ranchers."

"Ranchers?" Fashner laughed. "Two ragtailed ponies with hickory stirrups and one hungry mule with a straw collar. I hate to tell you, but you ain't wanted."

With great deference, Sennett said, "Where are you gentlemen from?"

13

"Alabama. The Black Warrior River."

That was a vague enough answer, Sennett thought. A polite, friendly answer, but sure as hell vague. The Black Warrior was a mighty long river.

"I'm from Alabama myself," Sennett said. "I was raised in the Tombigbee Swamp country. My name's John York Sennett."

They looked at him hard with their crystal-blue eyes, nodded, and looked away.

"We're glad to have you in the valley," Sennett said. "Don't judge us all by Mr. Fashner. His big mouth always swings its tailgate this way."

Fashner hunched, and faced him slowly.

To Sennett, the elder Durben said quietly, "Forget him. He don't aggravate us none."

"Why, it's Mr. Sennett," said Fashner mockingly. "The wise young man who owns a ranch and then won't live on it because there's too much gunpowder cracking off in that general neighborhood. Well, you come to the right place at the right time. These fine ranchers standing about you will soon be the new South Valley Association. If you want us to save that Anvil Pass of yours, you better join us."

"Not interested," Sennett said crisply.

Men pressed around him, many of them friends of his. Some looked hurt, some angry. Wooden-faced, he listened while they argued and reasoned with him.

"You own in the south valley," Fashner said. "But you don't hold with your neighbors. Is that it?"

"I hold with my neighbors," said Sennett coldly, "with these men, with their grass and their cattle. But I don't hold with you personally. I see you as you are, and you're exactly like Hatty himself."

Fashner was startled. "Me like Hatty? Why, I hate him, hide, hair, and bones."

"You're a beginner; Hatty's an expert. That's the only difference. You're both knotted up with a lust for power and a craving to dominate. These men are in distress and you're trying to grab them off for your own advantage. If they listen to you and let you lead them, in ten years you'll own their land and their hopes, and their sons will be eating your biscuits and meat and drawing your pay."

"So that's where you stand," said Fashner. His face was

14

lifeless, his voice muted to a bleak whisper. "I'm glad to know it."

"That's where I stand," said Sennett, and strode down the passage.

# 2

Beyond the passage mouth he came into an open quadrangle, blazing with sunlight. Here he got his saddled roan from a stableman. In the center of the yard was a well, with a wagonwheel windlass and a watering trough; three Browne riders were grouped by the trough, holding four mounts. He saw Ellen's fine bay mare, but Ellen was not in sight. Sennett spoke and they delayed their response to the point of insult. They looked defensive, sullen. He was in his saddle, walking his roan across the hard earth, when Ellen joined her men and they mounted swiftly. From behind him came a volley of hoofs and he was engulfed in horseflesh.

They cannoned up around him, and boxed him to a halt. The shoulder of Ellen's big mare breasted Sennett's roan to a stumbling turn, and Sennett flung himself about to face them in fury.

"Try that some time without a woman along," he said harshly to the riders, "and I'll show you an answer to it."

They were smiling, but their smiles were strained and unconvincing.

Flushed and determined, Ellen Browne said, "Mr. Sennett, I want to talk to you."

He waited in silence.

She said, "Mr. Hatty's still in town. You must look him up and tell him you've changed your mind."

Irritated, he shook his head.

"If you stay out, just at this time, it may be the fuse to explode the barrel."

"The barrel has other fuses. Holly Fashner, for instance," said Sennett, and told them of the meeting in the passage. They listened intently.

After a pause, Sennett said, "I don't understand you.

15

Your father is killed, by Hatty and here you are, galloping around, blowing the Hatty bugle."

"He was killed in a fair fight," said Ellen Browne.

Sennett had heard the story many times.

Sawyer Browne had been killed at twilight, in the passage he had just left. Sawyer had been talking to Dewey Chitwood, the stable owner, when a Hatty rider swaggered past them. Browne, hating all things Hatty, had quarreled with the rider and the rider had shot him. Chitwood, a neutral observer, had seen the whole thing. To Sennett it was the old, sad story of a man with more courage than skill provoking a fight and losing his life. The rider, one Buck Needham, was a transient whom Sennett had never seen; next morning he was gone.

The red-tan faces of Ellen Browne's punchers bobbed in earnest agreement.

"In a fair and square fight," one of them echoed.

Maybe so, Sennett thought. But there's more here than shows on the surface.

The girl grieved at her father's death, anyone could see that—and yet, at the same time, she seemed hostile to his memory.

Abruptly, she changed the subject. Rapidly, she said, "Mr. Hatty is the only one who can bring peace to the county. Things have been bad, but they can become much worse. You're a stranger, so you can't grasp the terror of a real range war. It goes on and on, whirling and swirling, getting bigger and bigger, until every man, woman, and dog is pulled in. No neutrals are acknowledged in range war territory. There'll be barricades behind cabin doors, line camp assassinations, Main Street massacres until the mountains shudder. We're simply trying to do the right thing, and no price is too high."

"The price is much too high," said Sennett, "but I have no hope of convincing you. Let me ask you this. What about Jim Trego?"

"Mr. Hatty says he must go. And I certainly agree."

Sennett regarded her curiously. "Jim tells me that in the old days he was almost an uncle to you. That he taught you to ride and shoot."

"Yes, he did."

"And that when you were a toddler he taught you to set a figure-four trap and made you cornstalk fiddles."

"Yes." She looked unhappy now, as did her riders. The men were showing wild shame in their eyes.

"But that was when you were a child," Sennett said. "Now you're through with him. Out he goes, eh?"

"Jim Trego is a troublemaker," she said steadily. "And this county has had enough trouble."

"Listen," Sennett said confidentially. "Why don't you get out of Hatty's North Association and forget Fashner's South Association. Come in with me on my Anvil Pass Association."

She was thunderstruck. "I didn't know you had your own private association."

"I don't," said Sennett. "That was just a joke."

He smiled grimly.

Cutting his horse in a small arc around them, he trotted it briskly across the brick-hard yard, through the open gate at the rear. A turn brought him into Main Street and after a few blocks he was on the county road. Setting a leisurely pace, he traveled southward.

In the distance, through the heat, shimmering uplands looped about him in a circlet of bronze. The grass of the rolling valley floor seemed endless. Once he saw a lonesome chimney standing amid charred embers. Hatty work. Later, about sunset, he passed the gulch mouth where the Wilkinses had been found in their buckboard. More Hatty work. The miles unfolded behind him and night came.

About eleven, he rode into his ranch yard.

The big house was dark, but yellow light fell from the open door of the bunkhouse. He had bought the ranch run-down and neglected, and had built it up with a small but competent crew. Several times he had offered the use of the big house to Trego, who dryly rejected it, preferring to bunk with his men. The ranch house, therefore, stood empty and was a sensitive point with the countryside. A rancher should live with his cattle and men and land.

At first, when Sennett arrived unexpectedly, as now, the crew had made a malicious flurry in settling him for the night, as though he were halfwitted royalty. He had long since put an end to that. Now Trego and a puncher named Wallace came from the bunkhouse to meet him, and he shook hands with them.

Jim Trego was a big man in his middle sixties, stooped and gaunt-cheeked, with hands like turtle shells. He had liked Sennett on sight, and they had become solid friends.

Wallace led away the roan. To Trego, Sennett said, "Bring the boys to the house, Jim. New things have been happening."

17

"The old things was bad enough," said Trego. "I'll find you some coffee." He ambled off into the shadows.

Sennett walked to the house and entered. He stood for an instant in the dark parlor, then lighted a lamp. The room was low and long, musty with imprisoned air. Along one wall were three casks of bacon sides and along another, on the bare floor, was a row of barn lanterns. He pulled up a thong-bottomed chair and sat by the table. In a few minutes they filed in, Trego, Beach, Wallace, and Zaragoza. The cook, McCrae, followed them, carrying a tray of food. With the exception of Trego, their manner toward Sennett was always inflexible, resigned. Sennett said, "Where's Johnny Flint?"

"At the Handcuff Creek line camp," said Trego.

"How is he working out?" asked Sennett.

Two weeks ago he'd hired young Flint, a tramp, at the insistence of Dove's father. He was still uneasy about him.

"Well, I'll tell you," said Trego. "He's a wizard at anything you set him to. He earns his pay, and double. But the boys simply can't stomach him."

The boys looked pained at Trego's frankness.

Eating as he talked, Sennett gave them a careful account of the morning's events, omitting any mention of Trego. Their faces became alarmed and angry.

When Sennett had finished, Beach, a lizard-eyed Pecos man who had lost three ranches of his own at cards, said, "I say go in with Fashner, and quick, but of course it's up to you."

"I don't think Fashner will do, Tom," Sennett said.

"You don't think? Well, you better make up your mind."

Trego's forehead went gray in the lamplight. "Mr. Sennett has made up his mind, Tom," he said very gently. "He's just trying to be polite, and you might take a lesson out of the same book. Furthermore, that ain't no way for a hand to speak to an owner. Or maybe you ain't a hand any more; maybe you quit, is that it?"

His tone, like soft lightning, said that any of them, all of them, could quit if they liked.

Beach grinned wolfishly, genuinely amused. "Oh, no you don't, Jim Trego. You don't hint me off no easy job like this'n. Do I talk too salty, Mr. Sennett?"

Sennett shook his head.

They filed out and Sennett, picking up the lamp, went

18

through a door into a small room. There was a dresser here, a chair, a cot with a buffalo robe on it. He undressed, blew out the light, and went to sleep immediately.

Things were well astir next morning as he crossed the veranda into the yard. Suddenly his small ranch was very beautiful, very important to him. Directly at his back door loomed the two scrub-and-rock peaks, Big and Little Anvil; northward the valley spread before him, lush and shimmering in the sun. The men were busy with pre-breakfast duties about the barns, and Sennett sauntered to join them. He wanted a private word with Trego, delicately warning him of his Hatty enemy, then breakfast and his departure. He was rounding the bunkhouse when a rider on a buckskin swung up to the corral gate. It was Johnny Flint. Three hands were in sight, but none of them greeted him. Sennett joined him, and Wallace and Zaragoza strolled up.

Johnny Flint was young, horse-jawed, and copper-skinned. His face was creased and his hair dry and black. Sennett had never seen him any other way than sullen. He had come to Napier unknown, had apparently appealed to Dove's father for a job. Mr. Stafford had shoved him off on Sennett. In no time at all he had become the talk of the county because of his wizardry with horses and cattle. Always he wore a scarf about his neck; at the moment it was a rag of blue cotton, but in town it would be fine yellow silk.

Suddenly, as he was unsaddling his horse he turned and said, "Mr. Sennett, I'm short of poker money. Will you lend me five dollars on my gun till payday?"

This was unheard of, and Sennett hesitated. Wryly, Zaragoza said to Wallace, "Hatty running crazy and he wants to pawn his iron."

Laxly, Flint drew the weapon from its holster; it was long-barreled, well kept, with a discolored walnut grip. Absently, he cocked it as he drew it and then, somehow, his thumb slipped and its throat let loose with a deep-bellied roar. The barrel was scarcely level at the instant, angling away from them, past the snubbing post in the center of the corral. Wallace and Zaragoza frowned at such carelessness.

Beyond the corral was the stackyard, with the winter

19

hay. Near the stackyard, partially hidden by a wagon, Trego was greasing an axle. Sennett, who was facing him, saw him go over in a limp heap.

Sennett shouted and ran toward him, and the crew clustered about him.

He'd been shot through the heart.

Two hours later, at breakfast, conversation still dwelt on one subject, the freakishness of the tragedy. It was the strangest accident they'd ever beheld, they all agreed. Only fate could have guided that little chunk of lead along such a remarkable channel, to strike a half-hidden target. When breakfast was finished, they went to the bunkhouse. Since Trego had left no kin, Sennett divided his effects among the unhappy crew. This done, he led them into the yard, into the shade of an ancient cottonwood. Here he named Beach as new foreman, and asked for objections.

The only objection came from Beach himself. "I ain't good enough for it," he said placidly. "But who of us is?"

Through it all, the burial, breakfast, the division of property, Flint had been in the background, expressionless, silent.

Now Sennett said, "One thing more. Pack your bag, Johnny, and get moving. You're finished here."

There was a murmur from the men, a faint sound of disapproval.

Old McCrae put it into words. "Be fair, Mr. Sennett. Maybe you don't like this young fellow, and maybe I don't neither, but accidents will happen. Remember, you're in the West. Out here most everybody carries guns and, naturally, there's a heap of gun-handling. Naturally, too, with all this handling, a gun fools you now and again and makes its own special trouble. I'd say this boy, right this minute, feels worse than any of us. It ain't no time to bear down on him."

"That's the truth," exclaimed Zaragoza.

"He's a mighty good worker," said Beach.

A man with a fine gun like that simply doesn't let his thumb slip, thought Sennett. I can't be wrong. He killed Trego deliberately, with miraculous marksmanship.

"Pay him what we owe him," Sennett said curtly. "And get him moving. I want him off my property."

Flint's head was turned aside, his chin tucked into the

hollow of his shoulder. He looked heartbroken, and Sennett, standing at an angle from the others, glanced at him. Sunlight caught the line of his jaw and the small, bunched muscle under his ear. He was smiling.

Sennett would never forget the sight of that secret smile.

Purple dusk clouded the street when Sennett returned to Napier, and golden lights gave the shabby little town a sleepy charm. He went to his hotel, to his room, and found a note on his bed. The handwriting was large, shaded, and flowery. *September 16th 11 A.M. Dear John: Would like to talk to you. Yr ob'd't & humble s'v't, Charles Aubrey Stafford.* When Dove's father put pen to paper, he always produced quite a document, no matter how slight the content. Well, thought Sennett, I want to talk to him too. I want to ask him a few questions about a tramp named Flint, questions I should have asked before. He bathed, put on clean linen, and went down into the lobby.

His hotel, the Napier House, was remarkably respectable. The lye-scrubbed lobby had three doors, one to the dining room, one opposite it to the adjacent stage office, and the street door. The street door was open to the dusty coolness of the autumn night, and townsmen, ranchers, and their families were relaxing in pleasant sociability. There were probably a dozen women present, and half that many children. As Sennett threaded his way to the door, three Hatty riders materialized before him, blocking his path.

A month ago these men had been strangers to the county; now they were well known, and feared. They were but three of many. Their leader, a dissipated curlyhead in batwing chaps, said loudly, "Sennett, I want to buy them boots you're wearin' How much?"

Sennett slowed to a stop. The room became silent.

"And that fancy vest. And that gold ring on your finger." The ring had been Sennett's mother's; it had been her wedding ring, and he was sure the rider sensed it.

The stillness in the room was now oppressive. Mothers hugged children to their knees.

The flanking riders moved now to the left and right, putting Sennett in position for crossfire. It was as though they had done this many times before.

"You're a peddler, ain't you?" said the curlyhead coarsely. "I've always heered a peddler don't care for nothing but trading and penny-pinching. He's a kind of a pig, ain't he, rooting around night and day, swilling down dimes and nickels and quarters. Correct?"

"Correct," said Sennett briskly.

A mother gave him a grateful glance.

Floundering a little at this unexpected answer, the rider said lamely, "Well, then. Name me a price."

"Twelve hundred dollars," snapped Sennet, in his most businesslike voice. "Cash on delivery, here and now. Let's see your money."

The room laughed, and the three riders, confused, wheeled and swung into the dining room.

The air pulsed with gratitude, but Sennett ignored it. Outside, on the boardwalk, his collar was wilted and his wrists were wet. Something had happened in the last thirty hours. The Hattys were after him now, out in the open.

And he'd almost shot his first man in a little over three years.

# 3

WHEN Sennett came into the center of town, Main Street was bright and noisy, well launched into its busiest night hour. Townsmen and ranchers chatted in shop entrances and the heavy air pulsed with dusty heat. Everywhere, along the sidewalk, in the saloons, he attempted to hire two new hands to fill the vacancies at Anvil; everywhere he met stolid refusal. The word was already out, apparently, and his name was calamity. He could see it in their eyes. They considered him a man in bad trouble, without friends, a man unable to protect himself. But there was more than this, he realized, for here and there he encountered something entirely new to him—restrained hostility.

Four ranchers, all serious, respectable men, stood in the entrance of the barbershop. As Sennett approached on his way to the Staffords', one of them said, "Just a minute, Mr. Sennett." The others studied him thoughtfully.

He had spoken to these men earlier, inquiring about hands, and they had barely answered him. Now, deliberately, he passed them, but came to a halt slightly beyond them.

"We hear tell you're forming an association of your own," the rancher said. "An Anvil Pass Association."

"Well, I'm not," said Sennett crisply.

"Anyways, that's what they're saying."

"I made the remark, yes. But I explained it was a joke. Forget it."

Ellen Browne had probably repeated it innocently. But once started, a rumor like that would spread like wildfire.

The rancher slowed his voice to a drawl. "They say you've been claiming you've got a mighty good thing in that pass. That when the railroad is finished every cow in the county will have to funnel through it and all you'll have to do is cut 'em through at so much per head—"

"Where did you hear that story?"

"Blackie, at the Billiard Palace, is saying so. He heard it from Holly Fashner."

So Fashner had picked up a harmless joke, had added to it, and had twisted it into a venomous attack.

Too tired to argue, almost too tired to deny it, Sennett said, "It doesn't even sound legal to me."

"Fashner says it is. He says if your pass was a river and you ferried cattle across, you could charge a head-toll. He says this is the same thing. He says you've got us."

Sennett's cheeks became hot and mottled. "I haven't any association, and I'm not going to form one. When they build the railroad and if and when they put a road through my pass, it will be a public pass, without toll or levy, free to any rancher that wants to use it."

The rancher smiled dryly.

"I see you don't believe it," said Sennett. "And of course you're welcome to your own opinion." He rubbed the heel of his hand along his jaw, and added, "But never express that opinion again to me, unless you're prepared to call me a liar to my face."

He could almost feel them turn to stone behind him as he walked away. He passed the Billiard Palace without even bothering to look in, crossed the street, passed through an alley by the harness shop, and came into Plum Street. He was quite sure that he was being summoned to the Stafford home to discuss his open opposition to Hatty. The Staffords, he knew, had a respect for the Hatty name

23

which was almost adulation. Furthermore, Mr. Stafford sometimes acted as Hatty's business advisor.

Mr. Stafford met Sennett at the door, and led him back to the study. This study, somehow, always made Sennett uncomfortable. It was pretentious and morose, in what Mr. Stafford supposed was the best Eastern fashion, with plum-and-bronze wallpaper and cumbersome black furniture. Lamplight glinted on muddy varnish and on the brass heads of carpet tacks. There was the suffocating smell of dusty lint and of medicated hair salve. When they were seated, Mr. Stafford leaned forward in his chair and shot his cuffs dramatically. Until Sennett had come along, he had been Napier's leading businessman. He was severe-looking, pompous, and plump in skin-tight pants. He said, "I understand Mr. Hatty made you a proposition, John, and you turned him down."

Sennett had a cheroot in the fork of his fingers, and was about to light it. He became suddenly motionless. "That's right," he said carefully. "I turned him down flat. It was the only thing to do."

"I couldn't believe it at first, but when I figured it out I couldn't help admiring you. Never take the first asking price, eh? That's mighty good business. Drive a hard bargain with him. Get him where you want him, and clamp down on him."

"I thought Hatty was a friend of yours."

"Oh, he is, he is. A close friend."

Sennett stared at Stafford silently.

Stafford chuckled. "The two of you will get together eventually, of course. And you'll make a great team."

"Well, thank you," Sennett said pleasantly. "Now there's a real compliment."

With a gluey smile, Stafford said, "Then, maybe, some time in the future, we might make it a three-way partnership. We could tie this old county's tail in a knot. This is no promise, of course; it's just something for you to look forward to."

"It is indeed," said Sennett.

"Three years ago," said Stafford, "after you'd been in town scarcely a month, I said to my wife, 'There's a whippersnapper floating around named John Sennett and I'd better keep my eye on him. He's money-crazy, and he's going to amount to something.'"

"Is that the way I act?" Sennett asked, interested. "Money-crazy?"

"Not act, are. And it's a gift, son."

His face expressionless and relaxed, Sennett considered. Could Stafford be right? He had lived his boyhood in semi-poverty, but it had been a happy boyhood. Hard, but happy. Then, at the end, had come that slow, man-eating illness upon his father with no money to provide ease for his father's last days. Little money, in fact, for the barest medical treatment. In those long and horrible days and nights, lack of money had become a black monster to him. His father had died, and had been buried beneath the cedar in the Sennett burying ground, but the monster in Sennett's mind did not die. Under the name of remorse, it grew. Without realizing it, he had been trying to wipe it out, too late, with an excess of zeal.

Changing the subject, he said, "I had to fire Johnny Flint this morning. Where did you ever dig him up?"

Stafford said, "Mr. Hatty dug him up. He showed up on Main Street, just a timid country boy, as I understand it, and Mr. Hatty felt sorry for him and asked me to get him a job."

"Any job at all, or a job at Anvil?"

"Anvil, Mr. Hatty said. Because it was so nice and peaceful. So many of the other ranches are having a little trouble. Why did you fire him?"

"His thumb slipped, and he shot Jim Trego."

Stafford's face went lax. He jammed his fat, liver-speckled finger into his mouth, and blurted, "How tragic!"

Sennett was sure he meant it. Stafford, like many others, had known Trego from the old days, and seemed to respect him. There seemed nothing more to say.

They sat in silence, smoking their black cigars, and the hot lampshade added its stifling odor to the musty, boxed-in air. After a bit, Sennett arose, said good night, and went into the hall. Dove was waiting for him by the parlor door, and they went out on the porch. Tonight she was dressed in frosty green and had a little bunch of velvet lilacs at her waist.

He was too harassed to talk, too weary and troubled, but he felt great comfort and excitement, standing silently beside her. His big knuckled fingers grasped the porch rail, and she laid her cool, small palm across them. Suddenly on fire for her, he tried to take her gently in his arms, but she moved lightly away. Once more he reached for her. But now she was passing gracefully in front of him, so that he caught her wrist only.

In this way, walking before him, and leading him with her extended arm and wrist, she took him down the porch steps, and around the corner of the house. The fire raged in him now, but he felt thwarted and muddled, blaming vaguely his own clumsiness, for her manner was provocatively tender and affectionate.

By the side of the house, in the dark night by the cellar door, were two rocking chairs. They had been placed so that they were close, yet distant, well divided from physical contact. With a lingering touch to his shoulder, she seated him in one, herself in the other.

She said, "I want to talk to you. I'm worried to death about you."

"Nothing to worry about," he said. "Nothing at all."

He made his voice carefully casual, even a little amused.

"Nothing? How in the world could so many people become angry with you so quickly? Not only Mr. Hatty, or even Mr. Fashner, but everybody. And you haven't done anything to them."

"Very true," said Sennett. He tried to soothe her. "Everything is going to be all right. How's the garden party coming?"

"Something very serious could happen to you."

"Oh, I don't think so," he said lightly.

"Take your bank, for instance," she said. "If people work up a lot of foolish grudges against you, they won't put money in your bank."

Fatigued, it was a moment before he knew what she was talking about. Long ago, he had told her about his dream of starting a bank. "The bank will have to wait," he said wearily.

"That was just an example," she said. "It's you we're worried about. Isn't it?"

"Yes," he said. "I mean, no." Stiffly, he got to his feet.

"I like Mr. Hatty," she said. "And I like Mr. Fashner, too. My father brokers cattle for both of them. You might say the very clothes I wear and the food I eat comes from them, and people like them. But it's you I trust and worry about. I love you and trust you all the way."

"I'm dead on my feet," said Sennett. "Good night."

She stepped behind him, kissed him quickly on the nape of the neck—and was gone.

When Sennett acquired the Napier House, he had taken two rooms on the second floor for his own use, a small

26

office overlooking Main Street, and a smaller room at the rear, a frugal cubbyhole, as a bedroom. There were two doors to the bedroom, one leading to the hall and another to an upper veranda which extended across the back of the hotel. On hot nights, such as this one, he left the veranda door wide open. He was an extremely light sleeper. Yet when Zaragoza entered, he came like a velvet shadow, entirely without sound.

Touching Sennett's shoulder, he awakened him, and said softly, "It is Hilario. Beach is below in the courtyard. This is a very bad thing we have to tell you."

Sennett swung himself upright on the edge of the bed. Zaragoza told his story.

They had been at the Handcuff Creek line camp, Beach and Zaragoza. There was a hoofmark before the cabin door which Zaragoza recognized—the hoofmark of a certain Hatty pony. A Hatty man had visited Johnny Flint, and Flint had received him as a friend, for they had eaten together. This had happened just before Trego's death.

"You see," said Zaragoza, his deep voice vibrant. "This was a messenger coming to Flint with an order to kill Jim Trego. Trego's killing wasn't an accident. Flint killed him on orders from Old Man Hatty."

"Flint is out of the county," Sennett said wearily. "Over the mountains and gone. You can bet on that. Tomorrow I'll ride out to the Hatty place and ask a few questions."

Zaragoza sounded delicately sympathetic. "But Johnny Flint is not over a mountain and out of the county. Now, at this moment, he is at the Pastime Saloon."

Sennett arose, and dressed in the dark. From his trunk he took the old gunbelt he had worn as a deputy back in Alabama. With Zaragoza, he went out to the gallery and down the steps. Beach was waiting in the shadows of the courtyard. Wordlessly, they turned out of the alley, down Main Street, Sennett slightly in the lead.

Main Street was deserted. On impulse, Sennett looked at his watch. It was twenty-seven minutes after three. The shops were dark and only the saloons were open, settled down to a slow business, sifting patches of golden light into the rutted street. As Sennett and his companions pushed through the doors of the Pastime, Sheriff Lytle materialized from the darkness of the sidewalk and entered with them. He didn't speak.

All but two of the ceiling lamps had been extinguished

and the broad, low room seemed cavernous. Six or eight men sat at small tables, sleeping, or playing cards, and a swamper sloshed about their feet with his mop and bucket of dirty water. Halfway down the bar was Johnny Flint, in a cone of light, talking with the bartender. Highlighted by the lamp he looked ugly and cruel, with his bony underslung jaw and lifeless black hair. About his neck he wore his fine yellow silk scarf, clasped at the throat with a Mexican topaz.

When he saw them approach, he unfastened his scarf, thrust the topaz into a pocket, and walked slowly forward. He was bandy-legged, slightly crouched, and incredibly supple. In his left hand he held the neckerchief by a corner, drooping.

The card players came to rigid attention.

Everyone, including Sennett, could read the signs. This was the style of that small select brotherhood—deadliest of all gunslingers—the neckerchief fighter.

Sennett had never seen one in the flesh before, but he had heard much about them. With the neckerchief fighter it was either kill or be killed; he left nothing to chance. His procedure was this: he snapped his cloth in the face of his opponent, taunting him to seize it; if his man, humiliated beyond restraint, accepted the challenge and grasped the cloth, the duel took place instantly, at that brutally short range. It was vicious, violent, and yet had all the surface appearances of equal and fair play. Some neckerchief fighters favored the bowie knife, and their advantage here was the average man's squeamishness to cold steel.

As Sennett and his party approached, Sheriff Lytle had advanced to the fore, obviously to prevent trouble. Flint came to a careful halt and the sheriff said, "Simmer down, Johnny, simmer down."

"Looks like this is going to be a busy night," said Flint, and snapped the sheriff on the cheek with the scarf tip. "Grab it."

The sheriff ignored it.

Three times, venomously, the silk lashed out and tore at the sheriff's face. He kept his hands stiffly at his sides. Breath went down his throat in a rasp and the cords of his neck stood out whitely, like rods of suet. He seemed terrified, but more than that, confused.

In an instant he would be a dead man, or forever branded a coward.

Sennett said, "How much did Hatty pay you to kill Jim Trego, Johnny?"

Flint turned his attention to Sennett.

He stared at Sennett a moment, listlessly, enjoying his hatred, then flicked the neckerchief. The tip of the silk caught Sennett on his lower eyelid and he knew from the surprising pain that its corner was weighted in the hem, probably with bullet shavings. Despite himself, he flinched.

For the past two minutes he had been considering the situation impersonally, almost mathematically, as though it were a problem in a ledger. Calmly, he had reduced it to these elements: Flint was no fanner, for a fanner required two hands. His skill, therefore, must lie in an unbelievably swift draw. The only method of defense, would be to obstruct that draw.

When the shotted silk struck Sennett's eye again, he seized it in an iron grip, slashing it down and to the left across Flint's right forearm. At the same moment he stepped forward, crowding Flint backward with his chest. Flint's fingers were already touching the walnut of his Colt when the silk jolted him, and he fumbled. Sennett shot him once, then twice more. So merged were the two men, pressing upright against each other in clothing and muscle, that only when Flint slumped did the watchers realize what had happened.

Faces in the room were dazed and hostile. Even the face of Sheriff Lytle was unfriendly. The grimy swamper, however, was radiantly happy. Beach and Zaragoza looked replete and comfortable, as though they had just finished a delicious meal.

Solicitously, Beach said, "Well, that's that. Now maybe you better get back to bed, Mr Sennett." To Lytle, he said, "We're going now. Care to walk down the street with us?"

"No," said the sheriff coldly.

Side by side, they left the saloon, went out into the early morning, and down the dark sidewalk to the Napier House. Beach and Zaragoza were self-consciously silent.

Sennett was silent, too, puzzling, worrying. Just what had happened there, at the Pastime? More than met the eye, certainly. In the first place, Flint was a hired killer and you could be sure he killed only on orders and payment. On orders and payment from Hatty. Yet he had challenged the sheriff before he had challenged Sennett. And, just as obscurely, how did the sheriff happen to be

29

on hand, at that very moment, expecting trouble? Did he have knowledge of the situation because, as everyone said, he was a Hatty man? And if he were a Hatty man, why had he been slated for a Hatty execution?

Next morning Beach and Zaragoza returned to Anvil, while Sennett rode out into the foothills, to talk to the two Durben brothers.

Their little ranch house, a miniature cabin of expertly squared logs, lay in a flat near a stream. Before its door, backwoods Alabama style, sat the two Durbens, barefoot, in the blistering sun. Sennett knew their names from hearsay; he greeted them formally as he dismounted. Willie, the brother with the silky mustache, was de-fleaing a monstrous yellow hound, and Hal was cutting rawhide bootlaces. They turned their eyes on him in quiet welcome. He realized they were not so old as he had at first thought; they were simply withered and tough and weatherbeaten.

The dog bounced forward, wagging its tail joyously. Sennett put down his hand to pet it.

"Careful," warned Willie. "He's getting all set to eat."

"But he looks so friendly."

"Don't he, though?" said Hal proudly. "That just proves he's part human. The friendlier he looks, the meaner he's feelin' He puts us in mind of our sweet, treacherous old granddaddy. Set down, Mr. Sennett. And thanks for backin' us up in town the other day."

"As though you needed it," grinned Sennett.

Hal went into the cabin. He returned with a jug, a glass of cold green tea, and three tin cups. Into each cup he poured tea, then rye whisky from the jug, stirring vigorously with his calloused finger.

Conversation was polite, but reserved. They discussed rain, dogs, their mutual Alabama homeland, and, eventually, the trouble in the county.

Carefully, Senentt brought up the purpose of his visit.

He said, "I'm short two men at Anvil, and I wonder if you'd work for me. But first, I want to explain the situation. I've been trying to do the honest thing but somehow I'm in a hornets' nest. One way or another, when you come right down to it, there's not one outfit in the county really friendly to me."

"So we've heard," said Hal graciously.

"Hatty has left me alone till now," said Sennett, "because there was no rush to gather me in and because he thought I might have a little influence in town. But that time is gone. Twice last night his hired gunfighters took a try at me. I've already had my foreman, Jim Trego, killed. And this is just the beginning. How does it sound?"

"Why, I guess it sounds all right," said Willie.

"Fine. Then you'll help me?"

"No," said Willie regretfully. "We hate to say it, but the answer is no."

"Why?"

"Glad to tell you," said Hal. "Working for somebody else has always been against our natural elements. I won't work for Willie, even, and he sure as heck won't work for me. That's the way we was bestowed on this earth, and it seems like nothing can't change us."

"Of course," said Sennett patiently. "I understand. Maybe I'm a little that way myself."

He swung into his saddle. They raised their hands in solemn farewell.

Turning due north and riding at an easy pace, Sennett passed through barren country, through endless acres of knobs and rocks and lifeless bush shimmering in a fiery sun. After a bit things got a little better, but not much, and he knew he was on Hatty land. Now he kept scrupulously in the open. Almost immediately two riders appeared, one erupting out of a slash, the other hammering down a hillside, and converged upon him. They were strangers to him, and he realized that Hatty had riflemen in reserve. Their clothes were foul, their hair well down upon their shoulders and matted, but their weapons were immaculate. One of them said, "You're on private property, Mr. Sennett."

This was a much different reception than he had expected. In the first place, they were extremely cautious, with no trace of contempt, and he surmised they had heard of Flint's killing and were laboriously trying to form a new opinion of him. Secondly, he had expected to be cracked at on sight while actually, in a surly way, he was being welcomed. "I'm headed for the house," he said.

"Well, we'll just ride along with you."

They didn't ride beside him, they rode slightly behind him.

# 4

THE HATTY ranch house sat in a bend of the old military road, with the mountains in the near distance behind it, upthrusting in boiling green foliage and dazzling snowy rock. Its crescent of outbuildings, once grand and showy, were squalid with neglect. The disease had spread to the house itself; everywhere was the blight of filth and decay. The center of the ranch house was two-storied, once painted an ugly mustard, now blistered and warped, with clapboards rotting from the joists and windowpanes cracked and patched with paper. Built out from the center structure, from left and right, were dingy one-story sheds, and across the entire front was an earth-floored veranda, its crude roof supported by unbarked poles. Here, in the stifling gray shade, on battered drawing-room chairs, sat Old Man Hatty and his son Todd, entertaining guests—Ellen Browne and her foreman. Sennett's escort wheeled off toward the barn.

Sennett walked his roan up to the group, dismounting just within the lip of shade and hitching to a stanchion, so that he and his horse stood brutally in their midst, almost in their laps. Fuming, he was surprised to see he was being received with smiles. Hatty's was merely a muscular contortion, Todd's was stubbled and sly, Ellen's was somehow grateful and earnest and relieved. Her foreman, however, a hulking old-timer named Ed Nestor, smiled not at all.

Old Man Hatty hunched forward in his chair, snapping his knee and elbow joints like a spider. His wizened face was cruel.

"Now, Mr. Sennett," he said, "before you open your mouth, I want you to get it through that hammerhead of yours just where you stand. I went to you like a gentleman and made you a gentleman's proposition and you turned me down. You insulted me and sneered at me, but I didn't expect much more because I judge a man as I judge a horse, on his breedin' Since then you've been thinking it over and for some reason or other you've changed your mind, so you come flying out to Old Man

Hatty and try to patch it up. This time it's you, unasked, that's making the offer and it better be good. Well, let's have it. What's your proposition?"

Now Sennett understood why he had been welcomed with smiles. They thought he had come to capitulate. At that instant, too, he realized some completely separate antagonism was taunting him, in a clouded corner of his mind.

It had been goading him since his arrival. Vaguely, all along, he had felt for some reason that it was Ellen, and now he tried to clarify it. She sat tall, erect, serious, watching him. His eyes went over her body and clothing. Her charcoal-black riding skirt was threadbare, her boots worn, her shirtwaist crisp and white. Nothing there. Her amber gaze was on him, drinking him up eagerly, helplessly, but certainly this was not his antagonism. Then he solved it. It was her hat.

And her hat was in Todd Hatty's hands. His hands were large and egg-shaped, with a glazed, speckled skin, covered with orange hair. Like the others, he was watching Sennett; and as he watched he rolled and rerolled the brim of Ellen's hat, in a gesture that seemed arrogant and possessive.

This is what has been annoying me, thought Sennett. But why should I be irritated because Todd Hatty feels possessive toward Ellen Browne?

To Old Man Hatty, Sennett said, "I'm afraid you're a little twisted. I wouldn't be caught in the same hog wallow with you. I haven't come to negotiate with you, I've come to warn you."

There was an instant of silence.

"Leave me alone," said Sennett quietly, "and leave Anvil alone. And this is the last time I'm going to say it."

In a quivering whisper, Old Man Hatty said, "You stand on my own land, at my very doorstep, and threaten me?"

"This isn't a threat. I'm just giving you some sound advice."

Nestor, the Browne foreman, looked interested. "This ain't none of my affair, of course, Mr. Sennett, but what did you have in mind?"

Sennett gave a wry laugh. "There you've got me, Mr. Nestor." He spoke as though there were no one else present. "It's come on me so suddenly that I haven't put

33

much thought on it and haven't really worked it out. He could be killed, of course, as he's had so many others killed, but that would leave Todd, who would have to be removed in the same manner. Or I could run them out of the county, both of them, but that would only mean that some other county, somewhere else, would eventually have the same sort of grief we're going through. I tell you, it's a problem."

Todd droped Ellen's hat in the dust.

Runnels of sweat streaked the grimy stubble of his cheeks. Thickly, he said, "Maybe you'd care to take this up with me personally, and right now?"

Sennett regarded him thoughtfully. "Why, certainly, if you're qualified to speak. I've always considered you a sort of overgrown puppy."

Todd came to his feet in a roll, and kicked out the chair behind him.

Ellen was terrified. "Don't, Todd," she begged. "Please."

"And another thing," Sennett said pensively. "If we had raised you back in Alabama, Todd, we'd have taught you how to shave. There's nothing to it, really, once you get the hang of it."

Todd crouched, jutted his neck, and spread his fingers. It was about the silliest spectacle Sennett had ever witnessed.

"I can't take no more of this!" Todd bellowed.

Old Man Hatty came into the picture. Sternly, he said, "Todd, Mr. Sennett, you youngsters cool off. I won't have this."

Todd looked tragically disappointed.

They'd put on this act many times before, Sennett thought. Todd blustering, the old man stepping in to divert a showdown.

Sennett looked quietly from one to the other, then glanced at Ellen, who was tense and ramrod-straight. He shrugged, nodded politely to Nestor, and swung into the saddle.

Five miles beyond the Hatty boundary, a rough wagon trail forked into the road; this trail led southwest, across the deserted Knutson ranch, terminating in a trace at the Browne ranch. When Ellen and her foreman returned, they would come this way. Within the fork was a boggy spring, green grass, and a few trees. Here Sennett grazed his roan, took cheese and biscuits from his saddlebag, and

34

settled down to wait. Within the hour Ellen and Nestor came into view, and pulled up beside him to water their mounts. They looked bewildered and unhappy, but showed unconscious pleasure at the sight of Sennett.

Without preamble, Sennett said, "You people have made a mighty bad move, throwing in with Hatty. With your Lazy B in his pocket he's going to rip this county to shreds. I'm asking you to break with him."

Nestor looked thoughtful, and Sennett took this for agreement, but Ellen said doggedly, "Mr. Hatty is this county's greatest power, and he must be made a power for good. Only through Mr. Hatty can all this bloodshed be ended."

"But it will work the other way," said Sennett. "Don't you see? Behind the shield of your respectability he'll really cut loose."

"I'm afraid we look at this two different ways, Mr. Sennett. I gave him my word to support him. And I refuse to break it."

Sennett stared at her, carefully wiping the exasperation from his face. He tried it again, indirectly. "I don't understand you, Miss Browne. Your father was killed by a Hatty man."

"He was killed in a fair fight," she said.

"Fair fight, fair fight," said Sennett impatiently. "You can't say anything else and the very words themselves are nonsense. Your father was an innocent amateur. This Buck Needham, you can be sure, was a professional."

She swung from her saddle to the ground, and Nestor followed her. Again, watching her, Sennett had the feeling that he had stirred up some deep, dark emotion in her.

An idea struck him, and shocked him, and he asked quietly, "Can it be you really didn't love your father? That, actually, you hated him?"

"I loved him," she said. "I loved him very much."

"Possibly you loved *and* hated him?"

Lazily, Nestor said, "Now that's no way to talk to a lady, my friend. Maybe you want to apologize?"

"That's all right, Ed," said Ellen. "Perhaps I'd better tell him the whole story."

With a warning grunt, Nestor tried to silence her.

Nestor was in his late sixties. He was known in three counties as a strange man, and potentially a dangerous one. He didn't smoke, drink, curse, or raise his voice in temper. Sennett suspected that his whole life was built about one obsession—a cold, almost insane loyalty for the Browne family and the Lazy B.

Ellen said, "My father was two different kinds of a man. One was pretty fine, but the other was not." She paused, then went on. "He went on drinking sprees. Not often; a couple of times a year, perhaps. And generally with Jim Trego."

"And you hated him for that?" asked Sennett, annoyed.

"Five years ago, before you came," said Ellen, "my mother caught typhoid. I sat with her, the doctor sat with her, Ed Nestor here sat with her. But when she died my father was in Napier on a two-day drunk."

"A lot of the old-timers have that whisky fever," Nestor said reprovingly. "I've explained it to you over and over."

"He was with Jim Trego," Ellen said.

"And you never forgave him for that," Sennett said. "Nor Jim Trego either."

"How could I?"

"I have an opinion on that," Sennett said. "But you wouldn't care to hear it."

Suddenly, he realized the internal torment and strain this girl had been living under, and a surge of misery came over him. He kept his face motionless, however, and his eyes shallow and unresponsive.

She said, "Jim Trego was a bad influence on my father. My father was violent when he was drunk. The very day he was killed, that very afternoon, I saw him about to enter the Pastime Saloon. I tried to scold him into going home with me, but he wouldn't listen. I knew he might be headed for trouble. Well, he got drunk, and picked a quarrel with that Needham man at the stable. His hand was unsteady, and he paid for it. It wasn't Needham that killed him. It was whisky."

Nestor stirred uneasily. "Like I've told you before, Ellen, part of what you say is true, part isn't. There's another side of it, and I think Mr. Sennett ought to hear that side, too. Sawyer used to get looping a couple of times a year, yes, but he always slept it off in town, and never gave anybody trouble. Now I've asked you this already, but I'm going to ask you again. Did you ever see your father violent?"

"No," she answered. "But Mr. Hatty has. Many times."

"Did you ever see him even quarrelsome?" Nestor asked.

36

Sennett said, "No. But Mr. Hatty has. Many times."

She went white with anger.

With deadly calm, she said, "Mr. Hatty is very considerate and understanding and kind. I don't expect either of you to realize that, but it's true."

She swung curtly into her saddle, and Nestor followed suit.

Lord, Sennett thought with compassion. She's living in a terrible, self-made hell. And no one, no one at all, can release her.

From the height of their saddles they gazed down on him. Both faces were calm, expressionless. Finally, Ellen spoke. "Why did you come to the West, Mr. Sennett?"

He told them the truth. "I got restless. I lived in a big swamp and suddenly, somehow, the swamp seemed to close in on me."

He could see them think this over, and it sounded sensible to them.

"Tell me this," Ellen said. "Why did you ever buy Anvil? You don't know a horse from a mule, really, do you? You can't enjoy ranching, because you don't even live on your ranch."

These were extremely personal questions. She was putting them to him casually, managing to give the impression that his answers were in some vague way a matter of public welfare; the feeling came to Sennett, though, that she was using Nestor's presence as a buffer and was simply expressing a personal curiosity.

He tried to answer this last question honestly, too. "I like stock and I like land. A couple of years ago Anvil was pretty sorry. Jim Trego came to me and suggested I buy it. I did. Jim picked a few good boys and they got to work on it. It seemed like a hopeless job but they broke their backs and built it up to one of the finest little spreads in the county. There's a story among the ranchers that I just consider Anvil merchandise. That's not true. I really consider it my home, but I've just been too busy to make the move."

Poker-faced, they made no comment.

Ellen said, "What was your occupation back in Alabama, Mr. Sennett?"

His patience was running out. "Back in Alabama," he said, "I was a schoolteacher." This was partly true. He'd been a full-time deputy to his father, part-time schoolteacher.

Nestor looked shocked.

"Schoolteacher?" said Ellen. "Well, in the last couple of days you've taken on quite a classroom."

"Maybe the schoolteachers back East are different," said Nestor hopefully. "Maybe it's just been the dregs we've been seeing. Maybe the schoolteachers back East are all gunfighters."

"No," said Sennett. "No, indeed."

"Then how did you kill Johnny Flint?" asked Nestor.

Sennett returned their gaze blandly. "It happened so fast," he confided, "I really don't know."

After a painful silence, Ed Nestor said, "You kill a neckerchief fighter, and you don't know how?"

"Of course I know how I did it, actually," explained Sennett. "I removed my pistol from its leather pocket-book—this thing here, you see—and jiggled this little thing down here, this thing that looks like a curved nail. That's the trigger; that detonates it."

They looked paralyzed, both of them.

Ellen said politely, "That's very educational, Mr. Sennett, and I hate to leave, but we've got a long way to go. Are you ready, Ed?"

Nestor nodded stiffly. They left at a gallop.

Purple September night, heavy with dust and hot, lay over the town as Sennett returned to Napier. He had turned his roan to the care of a stableboy in the yard of the Napier livery stable and was walking the short passage to the street when he heard his name spoken. This was the passage where Sawyer Browne had been shot to death. It was about sixteen feet wide, earth-floored, between the office of the livery stable and a feed store; overhead these two buildings were joined, making the passage a long, boxlike tunnel. At the moment it was very dark, its only light coming from an orange rectangle thrown across the earth by the open office window. It was from this window that Sennett's name had been spoken; he had just passed it, and the lamp had come on just after his passing. He came to a stop by a hay scale and glanced backward, diagonally, over his shoulder.

He saw that there were three men in the office, around the lamp on the table; half a dozen others came in and joined the group. Chitwood, the stable owner, was not present. The party, apparently a meeting of some sort, was made up of highly respectable south county ranchers, and was being dominated by Holly Fashner. He stood in their center, hulking, filthy, bespangled with his coin silver trappings, gesturing with that false, inflammatory excitement which he could assume so readily. Beside him stood his brother-in-law, King Damietta, a bearish, muscle-bound bully known for his brutal humor against helpless newcomers, drummers, immigrants, itinerant actors. Fashner and Damietta together, Sennett decided, could make a bad team. It was Fashner who had spoken Sennett's name.

He was speaking now. His voice trembling and breaking with indignation, he said, "In my mind, I don't know which is our worst enemy, him or Ellen Browne. Both of them are traitors to the south valley. She's switched to Hatty and betrayed us and he's maybe even deeper. He won't come in with us, with his friends and neighbors. I ain't too sure they ain't all working together somehow. Sennett, undercover, with Hatty and Ellen."

Damietta nodded in emphatic agreement, but others among the group looked restless and unconvinced.

One rancher said, "Sennett turned Hatty down."

"That's what I'm saying. So they put it to us. Maybe they ain't telling everything. Look at it this way. Hatty at one end of the valley, Sennett at the other, and what sits between them? A mighty dandy empire, if they can get their hands on it. Hatty's the meanest of the two, but Sennett's the smartest."

Fashner paused, swept his glance slowly over his audience. "Sennett's knotted up with a craving to boss. He knows the county is in bad trouble and he'll try to grab us off, one by one, if we don't stop him. He'll own our land and our mortgages, and in ten years, if we don't stop him now, we'll all be drawing his pay." This was the very accusation, almost word for word, that Sennett had made to Fashner.

"What shall we do?" prompted Damietta.

"Do?" yelled Fashner. "Break 'em up in little handfuls and take 'em as they come. One at a time. Apache style. Fight fire with fire."

"Not me," said one of the ranchers, and left. Several of the others followed him.

"Don't worry about them," said Fashner, in scorn. "We don't need 'em. All we need is ten good men."

As Sennett made his way to the Napier House, many of the shops along Main Street were closing for the night, and the boardwalk was largely deserted. He watched the shadows carefully as he walked, wondering who might strike first, and how. Would it be Fashner, or would it be Hatty?

Sennett's thoughts returned to Fashner. He was cannily planning his campaign. With almost any ten ruffians, well organized, he might make a very good showing indeed. If he struck hard and fast, always at the weakest, always avoiding the Hatty outfit—for he would avoid the Hattys despite his big talk—he could cut a quick and damaging swath. He would move under the banner of righteousness and soon decent men would swell his following. Already, it seemed, his power and importance were rapidly increasing. It was a touch-and-go gamble for him. Could he build up his position to one of influence and safety before the Hattys awakened to his design and came at him like an avalanche? Sennett doubted it.

Fashner's chances of survival were small, but stranger things had happened.

The lobby of the Napier House was empty as Sennett passed the desk. The clerk said, "Mr. Sennett, you have visitors in the ladies' sitting room."

The ladies' sitting room was at the rear of the lobby, under the stairs. It had a slatted, varnished door with a china doorknob; Sennett entered, wiping the perspiration from his jaw with a rumpled handkerchief.

The room was small, with a chair, a horsehair couch, and a marble-topped table. The Brussels carpet was new, and the wallpaper, of poppies and green leaves and cockatoos, was also new. The place was used mainly by women and children in stagecoach travel, and sometimes by local ranchers' wives as a town meeting-place. There was an odor of sachet, dry carpet, and wallpaper paste. Dove, fragile and exquisite in the golden wash of the lamp, sat on the sofa, her father beside her.

Mr. Stafford rose to his feet. "Good evening, John," he said pompously. "Beautiful evening, beautiful. I'll just step outside."

He left the room and the slatted door shut softly behind him.

Alarmed, Sennett asked, "What's happened? Anything wrong?"

Dove shook her head. "I just wanted to look at you."

40

"Fine," said Sennett.

He tried not to show his bewilderment. In the years he had known her, she had never visited him under such circumstances, so late at night. Uneasily, he studied her. There was something different about her, something in her face that he had never seen before. Her eyes were crystal and blurred, and her delicate rosebud lips sagged laxly open.

"Are you all right?" he asked.

Then she was in his arms, clenching him so wildly that he was stunned.

His first reaction was concern for her. He realized this was not illness or hysteria. She was giving herself to frantic, unrestrained love.

He enfolded her in a strong clasp. Tenderly, he bent to kiss her, to soothe her. Tight against him, she threshed in his arms.

Gently, he disengaged himself. She seemed so helpless, and so childlike, so beyond reason, he felt impelled to protect her. He was concerned with her future opinion of herself. She must not face a tomorrow in which she suffered from a humiliating memory.

It was when he had disengaged himself, that the afterimage came into his mind. When he had bent to kiss her, his glance had traveled over her shoulder, to the base of the closed door. There, on the carpet, lay the key. It was a big brass key, and its proper place was here on the inner side of the door, but in the keyhole. And there was something wrong with that key.

Now he turned and gave it his full attention.

It lay on the floor—but half under the door, where there was a sizable crack. It could have fallen to the floor, but it couldn't have fallen under the door.

He walked to the door and tried the knob. The door was locked.

She watched him silently as he made the test.

"Your father took the key with him as he left," Sennett said grimly. "He locked the door on the outside, and stuck it under the door. So we could have complete privacy."

"Yes," she said.

"Whose idea was it?" Sennett asked. "Yours, or his?"

"His," she said.

This answer had a strange effect on Sennett. He had believed in his heart, from the moment of discovery, that it *had* been a sly and devious trick of Stafford's. Had he

41

not asked the question, he would have always believed so.

Yet, though her answer endorsed his suspicion, her voice, defiant, contemptuous, and frustrated, denied it. Now he was convinced that the whole maneuver had been the product of her brain, and hers alone.

Quickly, she said, "We're engaged, aren't we? What is the harm in our being alone?"

This was certainly true, he realized. Then why was it so repugnant to him? Because it had been so clandestine, he decided. And because Mr. Stafford had been a party to it.

"John," Dove said desperately. "Listen to me. I want children, but I won't have them here, with all this shooting. How about this? You sell out and go to Denver. I'll come along later and we'll be married. Do you hear what I'm saying? I'm saying definitely that we'll be married."

Suddenly, he got the idea that all this had been carefully planned, but had got tangled. The door was to be locked, he was to be in her arms, and then, his defenses broken, he might have agreed to anything.

The ugly idea came and went in his mind, and he rejected it. He was so muddled, he told himself, that he could scarcely recognize his real friends these days. Now he was even turning on Dove and Mr. Stafford.

Nevertheless, experimentally and teasingly, he asked, "Married? When?"

"Soon," she said.

"How soon?"

"Very soon."

He grinned at her in pride and affection, and patted her gently on the shoulder as though she were a lovable little colt. "We don't have to go to Denver," he said quietly. "When Hatty simmers down, and Fashner simmers down, we'll have our children right here. This is a wonderful county." He hesitated, then said, "It might be true, as you said before, that my close association with your family might eventually hurt your father's business. If that's so, I'm sorry. I didn't ask for all this trouble, but now that it's caught me I see only one thing to do—work my way through it as honorably as possible. I'm sure that's what you want me to do, isn't it? Conduct myself like a self-respecting human being?"

"Of course, John," she said. She refused to meet his gaze. "I trust your judgment completely." Almost inaudi-

42

bly, she added, "But I did want children so much."

"We'll have them," Sennett promised. "In herds."

He unlocked the door. Out in the lobby, the clerk had left the desk. A dim night-light burned. Mr. Stafford dozed in a chair. As they approached, he floundered to his feet. "Have a nice little visit?" he asked breezily.

"Moderately," said Sennett.

Mr. Stafford blinked.

Dove said nothing at all.

When they had gone, he climbed the stairs to his room. Now, in retrospect, Dove's memory once more enchanted him, and once more she seemed to him a helpless, fascinating, emotionally upset child. He even felt a little friendlier toward Mr. Stafford. When you came right down to it, he told himself, they were the only people in Napier who really gave a damn for him.

In his room, he put them from his mind and went to bed, but was unable to sleep. For an hour he lay in the dark, tense and restless. After a bit, he got up, put on trousers, groped on the dresser for matches and a cigar, and wandered out on the veranda. Here he sat on a bench in the dark, and smoked.

This upper veranda had a narrow roof and a railing, and extended at second-story height across the back of the hotel. Stairs descended from it, down the wall of the building to a small rear courtyard. Moonlight was bright in the courtyard, glazing the packed earth with a pattern of milky green and lavender, blotched with jet shadows.

While Sennett smoked, two men rode into the yard on small, wiry ponies. One of the men was upright in his saddle, the other rolled slightly to his pony's steps, swaying. Abruptly, this man slipped to the ground and sprawled loosely on his back. Quickly, Sennett descended the stairs.

The man on the earth was Hal Durben, and his companion was his brother Willie. Sennett lighted a match. Hal was half conscious, and bleeding from the mouth. His face was a crisscross of welts, and there was an ugly welt on Willie's face, too.

"What happened?" asked Sennett.

"We changed our minds," said Willie. "We want to work for you."

"What happened?"

"Hatty."

43

# 5

That's right," said Willie. "Mr. Sennett, you got your-self two new hands. Me now, and Hal when he's mended. We'll work for you, as you asked, but we'll do it our way."

Sennett shook his head. "Oh, no. My way, or not at all."

From the ground, Hal mumbled thickly, incoherently.

"What's he trying to say?" asked Sennett.

"He's apologizin' because we didn't take up your offer when we was in better condition."

"Forget it," said Sennett. "We all have our ups and downs. Your brother needs a doctor. Can he walk, if we help him?"

"He wouldn't want nobody to help him," said Willie. "He can make it alone, if I sneer him into it."

He bent over Hal, said loudly and distinctly, "Now you just lay there easy. We're going to get a buggy and take you to a doctor." Under his breath, to Sennett, he said, "Hal thinks buggies is only for ladies."

In the dust, Hal bunched his body in a loop, and staggered to his feet. "Let's go," he said.

Sennett tried to steady him, but he fought him off. Clumped together in the shadows, Hal weaving a little, they left the courtyard, passed down a short alley, and came to Main Street.

The county's only physician, Dr. Maddox, lived two blocks from the hotel on North Main, in a two-story clapboard house built flush to the sidewalk. The front of the ground floor was a notions shop and drugstore; behind the shop, and entered from the side of the building, were two sickrooms, largely used for typhoid, diphtheria, or gunshot patients. Above, on the upper floor, lived Dr. Maddox and his wife. No light showed in the building as Sennett and the Durbens approached. The short walk had been made in utter silence. There had been no conversation, no explanation, no further mention of Hatty. Sennett knocked once at the side door; then once again.

Dr. Maddox answered their knock. He was a stocky, somber man, with flat, sandstone lips. In days gone by he had been offered the mayorship of Napier and had rejected it as a frippery; he had been offered the sheriffship, too, and had screwed up his face in annoyance. Now, wordlessly, he led them into a small dispensary, lighted a powerful gooseneck lamp, and got to work.

Twenty minutes later, he said, "This one here—" and pointed to Hal, "has three broken ribs, I'd say, a broken nose, and maybe a slight concussion. He'll have to stay in the back room for about a week, for observation. This one here—" he pointed to Willie, "has been bruised and fairly badly beaten, but I'd say it isn't the first time for either of them."

"It sure ain't," said Willie affably. "It sure as hell ain't."

"Care to tell me about it?" asked Dr. Maddox.

"Well, they ain't much to tell, Doc," Willie said. "Me and Hal is brothers, as you might have heard. We live alone. Time hangs heavy on our hands. Sometimes we get to tusslin' with each other, and one thing leads to another—"

"I'm a busy man," said Dr. Maddox, "and I need my sleep. Good night."

Sennett said, "Doc, I'm going to ask you a favor. I'm taking Willie back to Anvil. Hal will be here with you. That leaves no one at their cabin. They don't have much in the way of stock, but they have a little. Someone ought to take care of it for them. I'll pay the bill. Do you know anyone you could send out?"

"I'll send out Hammerhead, my nephew." Albert—Hammerhead—Maddox was seventeen years old.

"I don't think anything will happen to him," Sennett said.

"I know damn well nothing will happen to him," Dr. Maddox said carelessly. "Or I'll poison every damn waterhole in the county. Friend and foe alike."

They stared at him.

He produced a plug of tobacco, clamped off a hunk that would choke a cow, and said, "Now get out of here. I've got to get this man to bed."

Leaving the doctor's, Sennett and Willie Durben crossed the street and a weedy vacant lot, and came out on Congress Street. They passed two offices, a saddle shop, and arrived at the glimmering yellow front of Sennett's big

45

store. He took out a bunch of keys on a rawhide thong, unlocked the door, and they entered. He pulled down a big-bellied lamp suspended from the ceiling and struck a match to its wick, elevating it.

They were in the hardware department. Through an arch at the left was the drygoods department, with its bolt goods and finery, and through a second on his right, groceries and staples. All around them were kegs of nails, plows, trace chains, axes. Behind a counter was a rack of Winchesters and Sharps—some pawned and unredeemed, some new—and a case of dull gleaming revolvers.

From this case, Sennett took a .45 and laid it on the counter. He told Willie, "Compliments of John York Sennett. You might need it. Don't shoot yourself."

Durben grinned solemnly and loaded it from his belt, leaving a chamber empty. He slipped it twice in his holster, half in, half out, expertly, to catch the feel and set of it, and nodded. "I've seen better and I've seen worse," he said. "Thank you kindly. I hope it pays for itself."

"For self-defense only," said Sennett. His voice was hard. "I want that clearly understood."

"Naturally. Naturally."

"And now," said Sennett, "I'll try it again. What happened?"

The whole story came out this time, and it was a brutal and vicious one. Hal and Willie Durben had been on their way home from town when five Hatty riders billowed out of the mouth of a draw and swamped them. The leader of this party, Durben said, was a mean curlyhead in bat-wing chaps who disarmed them, and stood them back-to-back.

"Say door," he'd ordered.

When Hal had said, "Doah," Curley had lashed him with his quirt.

"I loathe an' despise a Alabama accent," Curley had snarled. "They's only three polecats in the county uses it, and I aim to break you of it, all three. Say forty-four."

"Thutty-six," Hal had said. "Us Durbens is mighty poah in arithmetic."

"Mighty what?"

"Poah. None of us is scholahs. Thutty-six and fohty-foah is all the same to us."

Slash, the quirt had gone; slash, slash.

"Talk human!" Curley had raged.

"He tried me next," Willie said. "On sparrow and

shearer, and a couple of other Yankee tongue twisters, and began using the quirt butt on us. Hal got it worst. You see, from the very start Hal took stubborn and started talkin' such flat Alabama that even I couldn't understand him. They finally beat us to the ground, kicked Hal around a little, and left us there. We made it in to you."

Dry-mouthed in fury, Sennett said, "They're angry with me, so they take it out on you. I owe you Durbens a lot."

"You don't owe us a thing," said Willie. "If you'll just shake hands with me."

Sennett grasped the outstretched hand with a clasp of steel.

"That hand ain't been shook for twenty years," Durben said dourly. "And I doubt if it'll ever be shook agin."

As Sennett hauled down the lamp to extinguish it, he took a look about him, at the well stocked shelves, and aisle tables piled high with attractive merchandise. At the cloth and tin and leather and hemp; from New York, from Frisco, from China, from Europe—merchandise that had traveled by clipper and rails and mule train, over mountains, across deserts, through hostile Indians. Until this moment, it had filled him with a glow of accomplishment, just looking at it.

For a strange, opaque second it seemed dross, and unreal.

His mind was torn with people. With the Durbens, and Ellen Browne, with Hatty and Fashner, with the memory of Dove tight in his arms. This was a world of people, he realized, and there was no escape from it in things alone, no ultimate tranquility.

"Let's head for the hotel," Sennett said at last. "And start for Anvil in the morning."

"Suits me."

Sennett put out the lamp. In the dark, in a daze of preoccupation, he said, "Trouble, trouble."

"That suits me, too," said Durben.

It was sundown, next day, when they rode into the Anvil yard. Durben was given a bunk in the bunkhouse. Sennett had supper in the cookshed, for the first time joining his crew at their table. His avoidance of this in the past had not been due to snobbishness, but to the very reverse. They were a tight, complete little unit—tolerant of him, but wary—and he was oversensitive about intruding. In this manner the barrier of isolation had grown until it had seemed impenetrable, until tonight, when McCrae said self-consciously, "If you would eat with us, John, your biscuits would be hotter."

John. Not Mr. Sennett.

"And you'd save me a lot of steps," old McCrae went on. "Walking back and forth across the yard, and such."

"I'd like to," Sennett said. "I'd have done it before but I didn't want to break in on you."

"We knew it all along," McCrae said moodily. "I swear, Mr. Sennett, you ought to line us up and kick us."

Now it was Mr. Sennett. If there was anyone to be kicked, it was Mr. Sennett.

Talk at the table had been tense and excited. Beach and Zaragoza had brought back the story of Sennett's killing of Flint, and they discussed it in detail. They had information for Sennett, too. Riffraff from the Fashner group had been going about the south valley, talking friction against Anvil and Lazy B. Sennett told them about the Durben beating, and they listened indignantly.

He went to bed that night sensing a faint and cautious respect in them. It was pretty faint, and pretty cautious, but it was a start.

Morning sun flamed in the knobs of Big and Little Anvil, high behind the house, when Sennett, after breakfast and a smoke, made his way to the barns. Beach hailed him genially from the corral and he saw that Zaragoza was with him, and three horses were saddled, including his roan. Coming up, he waited for an explanation, and Beach said, "I just come in from Hominy Creek. I seen a little something I want you to take a look at. Hilario, too."

Hominy Creek was the Browne-Sennett property line.

"These are ticklish days," said Sennett. "It's no time to be riding a boundary—any boundary—alone."

They mounted, wheeled, and left the ranch yard at an easy gait, bearing northwest.

Soon they were in the thickets of the foothills and, after a bit, they struck, and followed, an ancient Cheyenne trace. Pressing them on their left were the looming, wooded knobs, sometimes cupped with sudden hollows, cool and shady and secret; sometimes sliced with bare, hot rock, scissoring off the sky. On their right was stony detritus and sun-baked scrub and matted saplings. The trail turned, and there was Hominy Creek, clear, flat and shadow-mottled.

From his saddle, Beach pointed. Sennett and Zaragoza followed the line of his lumpy finger. Midstream, an up-thrust of leaf-rock had caught a patch of drift, dead leaves and twigs. It was this patch, slightly disarranged, that Beach was indicating. "A horse," he said. "And heading upstream."

"One only?" Sennett asked.

"That's as far as I can go," said Beach. "It ain't me that's half hound-dog, it's Hilario."

"How many?" said Zaragoza. "That is very hard to tell."

Sennett asked, "How fresh?"

"Very fresh. I don't like this thing, boss."

"Nor I either," said Sennett.

No Anvil rider had left this sign, no Browne rider, no simple trespasser. It had been left by some sly horseman going to great pains to conceal his trail.

Zaragoza waded his mount to the farther bank, and they moved upstream. Shortly after, he raised his arm. They crossed to join him.

They were now on Browne land. Horsemen, and more than one, had emerged here.

"Four," said Zaragoza. "And one I know, for I have seen it hitched at the St. Louis Billiard Palace. It is Culp Fashner's blaze-faced sorrel." Culp was Holly Fashner's brother. "These are Fashner men."

Sennett said, "To get here by daylight, they must have started at one or two in the morning." He could see them in his mind: four men, slipping off in the black of night to a long hard ride and secret work.

"What are they up to?" asked Beach.

"Meanness," said Sennett. "And maybe worse."

Beach thought it over. "Well, we can't have none of that," he said blissfully. "Let's go!"

Unhappily, in a whisper to himself, Zaragoza said, "I know a second of these horses also." But no one heard.

Before them extended a leafy tunnel, an old logging road. Down it, the trespassers had left their sign. There had been no effort at concealment here, and the Anvil men followed it without difficulty. They'd covered scarcely a hundred yards when Zaragoza reined up. "Now I see five horses," he announced. He retraced, studying the ground. "Yes. Here they were joined by a fifth—a Browne man, it could be, for there is a Lazy B line camp just north of here."

"A traitor in the Lazy B," exclaimed Beach in disgust. "Now there is something I never hoped to see."

Sennett said, "Maybe he's no traitor. Maybe he just ran into them. Maybe he's a prisoner."

They broke into a gallop, and then into a dead run.

Ahead of them, in the near distance, a shot whanged out like a muffled whipcrack.

# 6

THAT SHOT told them two things. From the sound itself they knew it had come from a rifle, not a pistol. And from its direction, and nearness, they pretty well judged its probable place of origin. Simultaneously, the thought flashed through their minds: the old Cheyenne County Sawmill.

It presented its puzzle to Sennett, too. There had been just the single shot, with none following. This certainly couldn't be an attempted rescue.

Had the prisoner, then, been shot down either in escape or cold blood? Unlikely, Sennett decided. He would be closely guarded, and a sixgun would have been the natural weapon under such circumstances. But that rifle had been fired deliberately.

The logging road bent suddenly to the left, and they burst into a tiny hollow in a notch between two hills. It was little more than a pocket and the looming hillsides seemed to hang over it, seemed to tent it in arched branches and interlaced foliage. Immediately upon them, as they emerged from the road mouth, were the ramshackle buildings of the long abandoned sawmill. There were four of these buildings, office, bunkhouse, small cookshed, and the mill itself, mouldering and rotting, split with wild-grape tendrils. The air was musky cool, and heavy.

Sennett and his companions came upon these structures from the rear at full speed, passed between them, and smashed into the clearing beyond, their Colts in their hands.

Instantly, they were in a hornets' nest. Frantically, with a braking of hoofs and keening of leather, they churned to a stop.

Beach threw himself to the earth, lighting in full poise and balance, like a flung cat. Sennett and Zaragoza swung down beside him.

Here the fronts of the buildings formed a rough U. A couple of dozen yards away, tied to a rack before the old office, were four mounts, three belonging to the Fashner outfit, one to Lazy B. Loosely clustered about the Anvil men, a short distance away, were Culp Fashner, two of Holly Fashner's punchers, and Ed Nestor.

Nestor stood calmly in their midst, frail shoulders ramrod-straight, hands clasped quietly behind his back. His gunbelt hung from the crook of Culp's elbow.

Sennett's enraged glance took this in at a sweep—and it was then he saw the unbelievable.

Through the center of the little hollow was a small brook, motionless, pooled to cobalt and silver in the black-green shadows. On the bank of this brook lay Sennett's second favorite horse, Jefferson. Dead, in Sennett's second-best saddle.

Jefferson explained the rifle shot.

This was the mount and gear Sennett kept in reserve in town, at Chitwood's livery stable. At this very moment Jefferson should be in Napier. He had been brought to here, riderless, for his execution.

"Don't move, you skunks," said Beach, and added instantly, "unless you want to." He sounded so eager and merciless that Sennett flicked him a quick glance.

The intruders stood frozen. One of them had half drawn, the others, intent on business at hand, had been caught flatfooted.

Nestor said, "Good morning, Hilario, Tom, Mr. Sennett."

Culp dropped the gunbelt. He was a great hulk of a man, repulsive, ape-jawed. No one in the county seemed to know much about Culp Fashner. He had come to the valley shortly after his brother had arrived, and lived in a small hut on Holly's land. He rarely came to Napier. Rumor pictured him as silent and cruel. He was said to wear no guns, at least not in sight, and that in itself was somehow disturbing.

Now, Sennett noticed, Culp Fashner wore a gun. A

51

single .45 in the front of his waistband, in a belly-holster. Its wooden butt showed three sweat-stained notches. Gun notchers existed, but they were rare. In the eyes of decent men—and most outlaws, for that matter—they were considered the scum of the earth.

Nestor stepped forward and turned, presenting his back. His hands were tied together, cruelly, by the thumbs.

Sennett freed him with his penknife.

Nestor said, "They picked me up on the trail and brought me here. They were going to kill me, of course. They explained it to me over and over. Kill me, and Mr. Sennett's horse, and leave us so we could be found—to set Lazy B against Anvil."

"I see," said Sennett. "Which one of them shot Jefferson?"

"Culp," said Nestor. "With my Winchester."

A moment ago, Culp's two accomplices had been sullen but belligerent. Now they were stiff and subdued. All fight had gone out of them. Something had them badly scared. They had reason to be worried, of course, but they were more than that. They were paralyzed.

Nestor's gunbelt lay on the ground at his feet. He made no move to retrieve it. No one, in fact, made any move whatever.

"All three of them were in it," said Nestor. "But Culp is the head man. This is between him and me."

Ignoring him, Beach said to Culp, "What's them things on your gunbutt?"

Culp inhaled raggedly, but remained silent.

"Answer me," said Beach.

Unsteadily, Culp said, "Notches."

"You mean dead men?"

"Yes," said Culp, and Beach slapped him.

It was a slow, hard slap, loaded with contempt, and punishing, full across the mouth. For an instant Culp's lower face shone pale and bloodless beneath the impact, as though it were dusted with flour. Deliberately, Beach spat on his palm to cleanse it, and wiped it across the seat of his pants. They made a strange pair, little Beach, and Culp a good six feet four.

The two Fashner punchers, one named Morgan, the other Parrish, were casually known to Sennett. Parrish, a scabby-faced scarecrow, said carefully, "Mr. Sennett, things are happening you don't know nothing about. You mean well—I hope—but right this minute your men are fooling you. Why didn't they disarm us? Because it's going to look better this way. No matter what we say, no matter what we do, they're going to find some little excuse and wipe us out. It's been in their minds from the beginning. Not one of us three, except maybe Culp, is going to leave this place alive."

A silence fell, and grew. The pressure mounted.

Sennett said, "Is this true, Hilario?"

Zaragoza pretended not to understand.

"Tom?" asked Sennett.

Beach answered indirectly. "If anything gets out of control, keep sharp."

"Nothing is going to get out of control," Sennett said.

Now, all at once, Sennett was more interested in his two companions than he was in the marauders. He had smoked with these men, and ridden with them, but as they stood spread-legged in the blotched sun and shadow they were strangers to him. He remembered that Jim Trego had selected them, and they would have Jim's code.

They would be concerned with Nestor's capture and close escape, but not too deeply, perhaps. Jefferson, stolen, murdered, would be a different story to them. In their eyes this was an atrocity completely unpardonable.

Ellen Browne's words echoed in his memory. *There will be massacres.* He made his decision. This little hollow must not be filled with roaring carnage.

First, however, he made one more try. Reasonably, he said, "Tom, Hilario, listen to me. Make no mistake here. Handle this thing according to the law."

"Law?" Beach said politely. "What law? Oh, you must be referrin' to the cavalry across the mountains at Fort Riggs."

To Nestor, Sennett said, "You're a real longhorn, Mr. Nestor, and these boys of mine respect you. Maybe you can calm them down."

Nestor gave a mirthless smile. "Not me, Mr. Sennett. They're growed. They know right from wrong. I only wish I had my gun in my hand and was standing beside them."

Slowly moving his wrist, Sennett thrust two fingers of his left hand into a vest pocket. They came out with a tarnished badge, a small nickel star.

Culp slid his watery eyes at it. All of them saw it, and

53

all of them stared. Slowly, Sennett returned it to his pocket.

"That's the law, Tom," Sennett said pleasantly. He had the conviction that he was alienating himself irrevocably. "It worked back in Alabama," he said, "and maybe it will work here. Of course it's a little out of its territory, and its authority has long since expired and isn't worth a damn, but I think I'll stand behind it just the same."

There was a moment of stunned silence.

Culp Fashner broke it. Relieved now, feeling suddenly a sense of security, he said, "I eat them things."

Sennett ignored him. Still relaxed and affable, he said, "Now I'm dropping their gunbelts. And I don't want any trouble from anybody. You must get that very clearly. Then I'm taking them into Napier. If any of you still feel friendly enough to me, I'd like you to come along. If not, I'll deliver them alone."

Promptly, Beach said, "We're with you, John. There'll be no trouble." It came hard, but he said it.

Zaragoza simply nodded in agreement.

"Good enough," said Sennett.

Now that he had come through it, the backlash of tension hit him. For an instant he had lost them completely and now they were with him again. Truly with him, he felt, and more firmly than ever. Carefully keeping his face emotionless, he stepped forward.

He moved first upon Culp, considering him the most dangerous of the three marauders, approaching him from the side, keeping himself clear of any emergency fire from his own men. And somehow, as he approached, almost against his will, his gaze seemed unable to leave those ugly notches on that walnut gunbutt.

He said, "This is a wanted man. You can bet on it. If Sheriff Lytle will riffle through a few flyers he'll find this man is money to him."

Culp's hands, palms outward, were raised shoulder high. Sennett's hand was at Culp's waistband, reaching toward the belly-holster, when Culp's big left fist swung down, and into his flapping deerskin vest, into his armpit. His oily eyeballs seemed to protrude and his mouth contorted spasmodically. As he drew his second weapon, he shifted, placing Sennett as a shield between himself and the others.

Sennett fired at him, but it was Beach, six yards away, who killed him. Beach's Colt roared first, Sennett's blending into it.

As Culp crumpled to the ground, a cut-down .45 rolled from his limp fingers. It seemed all cylinder and blunt, gray bullet-noses.

Under Zaragoza's gun, Nestor unarmed Parrish and Morgan, pale and shaken.

"I knew he was up to devilment," Beach said. "And I was waiting for him. You put his back to the wall when you said he was wanted. He was a good five inches taller than you and his big old head, sticking up over your shoulder, was about the size of a nice, rotten watermelon. When I can't hit a watermelon at eighteen feet, I'll stop burning powder. You going to count this against me?"

"I'm going to count it for you," said Sennett. "And I don't think I'll ever forget it."

"Well, that's the way it is," Beach said philosophically. "You never know. If I'd have kilt him three minutes earlier, you'd have scalped me."

Nestor said, "You knew he had a second gun, Tom?"

"I guessed it," said Beach. "I didn't want to say it aloud, less I stampede him. I once saw a fellow down at Yuma with the same trick. In a way, you could call that notched gun a decoy. The notches stood for real dead men, I'd say, but they were actually earned with the short gun. You see when a man is wearing a notched gun you can't seem to keep your eyes off it, and you're wide open. Culp did it like that Yuma fellow. Fooled 'em with his belly gun and blasted 'em with his shoulder gun."

Across the hollow, a small path entered the clearing from the north. Now, out of this second trail, and into the clearing, rode Ellen Browne and four of her Lazy B hands—drawn, Sennett realized, by the sound of the shots. Later he learned they had been on their way to Hominy Creek and Anvil, for a visit with Sennett himself. They trotted their horses briskly through the lush grass, wading the brook, passing Jefferson, and joined the group about Culp's dead body. Sennett and Nestor explained the situation.

The Lazy B punchers listened in furious, tight-lipped silence. Ellen listened in silence too, disturbed but steady.

When the story had been told, Ellen said, "So back in

Alabama you weren't a schoolteacher, but a sheriff, Mr. Sennett."

"That was my father's badge," said Sennett.

Beach looked skeptical at this. Morgan and Parrish, too, looked unconvinced.

"We were on our way to your ranch house," she said, "hoping to find you. I've come to a decision."

She stood before him, beautiful in her anxiety, high-breasted and proud. This, he realized, was a fine pride, without arrogance. And her anxiety was not for herself but for others. Again he knew that here was a girl in torment, trying to do the right thing. But I'm trying to do the right thing too, he thought. And by God, I'm going to do it.

"But first," she said, "we want to thank you, all of you. You saved Ed's life. That terrible Holly Fashner. We shall always be deeply grateful—"

"That decision you wanted to talk to me about," said Sennett. "What was it?"

She looked at him full and hard, through the turbulence of her mind. "This," she said. "I've decided to buy Anvil."

Even Parrish and Morgan showed interest.

She said, "Mr. Hatty says that much of the valley's unrest is actually centered on Anvil. Every rancher in the valley, he says, is worried about you, and the railroad, and your pass, and what you're planning to do about it. I believe I've worked out an answer. I'm going to take Anvil off your hands, and add it to Lazy B. At a liberal price, of course."

And she could well pay a liberal price, Sennett knew. Sawyer Browne had been one of the wealthiest ranchers in the county.

Bone-tired, his eyes red-rimmed, Sennett rubbed his cheek and jaw with the back of his hand.

Everyone, it seemed, was trying to move him someplace. Dove, to Denver. Ellen, anywhere, as long as it was off Anvil.

His temper frayed past endurance, he said, "How can you say a thing like that? Anvil is not for sale."

Stiffly, she asked, "Why not?"

"For several reasons. Here's one. Hatty controls Lazy B. I don't want him sneaking into Anvil too."

The Lazy B riders stirred restlessly beneath the insult.

In a growl, Nestor said, "Watch your words, young man. Nobody controls Lazy B but Ellen Browne."

"And who controls Ellen Browne?" snapped Sennett.

Quickly, Zaragoza said, "Let's don't hurt nobody's feelings, John."

The prisoners had been lashed and mounted. Beach said, "Let's be on our way. We've got to get these men in to Napier. Let's go."

# 7

THE TRIP to town was stifling, oven-hot.

In the hollow, they left Ellen and three of her punchers; the men would take care of Culp, Jefferson, and Jefferson's saddle.

The little group rode single file, Nestor and one of his hands taking the van, Morgan and Parrish, once more tough and cocky, in the center, Sennett and his companions bringing up the rear. They rode with greatest caution, always alert for a delivery attempt by Holly Fashner, or a sudden assault from Hatty. This last could be the worst.

Sennett could imagine Hatty storming in, taking over, butchering Anvil men, perhaps, and hanging the prisoners. It would be a wonderful setup for Hatty to administer his particular brand of justice. And it offered a fine opportunity for Hatty's particular brand of sideline accidents.

However, nothing happened. The sun went down and a smoky silver moon climbed over the eastern hills. The low scrub on the black valley floor became an icy blue in the moonlight, and the air chilled. A little before eleven the lights of Napier showed in the near distance, through the purple night dust, and soon they were walking their mounts down Main Street, down Court Alley behind the courthouse, to the jail.

Sheriff Lytle lived in a small cottage facing Spring Street. Its rear abutted the county building, divided from it by the alley, and it, too, was county property. Its two front rooms, those on Spring Street, were bedroom-parlor and kitchen; the rear of the building, on the alley, had two rooms, too, a small entry office and an eight-by-twelve cell, with a blacksmith-made iron-barred door, the door-frame reinforced by flattened wagon rims. The office was empty as they crowded in, with a night lamp burning low on the battered rolltop desk.

Sheriff Lytle came along the passage from his kitchen, and joined them. He was barefooted, in broadcloth pants and dirty undershirt. Sennett had never cared much for Lytle, but now, for an instant, he scarcely recognized him. Abruptly he realized that the sheriff, not a drinking man, was drunk. Not active, energetic drunk, but foggy, listless drunk. He held it well, though, and Sennett doubted if any of the others were aware of it.

Brusquely, Nestor said, "Salt these two away, Lytle."

Without question, Lytle obeyed.

As Lytle locked the cell door, he asked diffidently, almost as an afterthought, "What charges are you preferrin', Ed?"

Laconically, Nestor related the morning's events, his capture, Jefferson's death, Culp's death.

"I'm preferring trespassing charges," Nestor said. A thing, of course, unheard of in Cheyenne County. "They'll come up tomorrow before Maddox." Dr. Maddox was the magistrate. "I'll appear and probably drop charges. I want them out of jail as soon as possible."

Out of jail and into eternity, thought Sennett.

"Then why charge them at all?" asked Lytle, perplexed.

"It was his idea," said Nestor, jerking a thumb at Sennett. "He loves law and order."

Blearily, Lytle scrutinized John Sennett. "Well," he said. "I guess that'll be all. Good night, gentlemen."

"I've got a little charge to make myself," Sennett said carelessly. "Remember, they stole my horse." This would put Lytle in a quandary, he knew. Lazy B had spoken, and Lazy B, a tremendous force in itself, now coupled with Hatty, would seem to Lytle absolute.

When Lytle failed to respond, Sennett said, "Lazy B wants these two men on the street, and you know why. To me Parrish and Morgan are lower than gophers, but it's not a question of that. I, too, am an injured party. I'll collect my justice across a judge's bench."

Beach and Zaragoza listened, attentive but noncommittal.

In drunken dignity, Lytle said, "I don't see how I'm in a position to accept that charge, Mr. Sennett."

"Who do you think you are?" Sennett asked. "Judge Maddox?"

"Culp stole your horse and killed him. Anvil killed Culp. That's that. This here is other business, Lazy B business."

"You're so drunk your knees are spraddled," Sennett said in disgust.

Rage twisted Lytle's face. "I've had about enough of you, Mr. John Sennett," he shouted. "Mr. Hatty's trying to calm this valley down, Miss Ellen Browne's trying to calm this valley down, and you and Holly Fashner go about stirring up bad feeling. I used to like you, but it's got so I can't stand the sight of you."

Sennett nodded. Unfastening his vest and shirt, he took three gold coins from his money belt, two double eagles and an eagle. Fifty dollars. Thoughtfully, he laid them on the desk.

"What's that for?" Lytle asked suspiciously.

"For you," Sennett said. "You've earned them. It's worth fifty dollars to me to know you're my enemy."

Face expressionless, he turned to Nestor.

"How about you?" he asked the Lazy B foreman. "You got some money coming too?"

There was a deadly hush.

"No," Nestor said slowly. "I ain't got none of your money coming. I'm not your enemy." A faint, wary smile curled the upper rim of his lips. "And I ain't exactly your friend, either," he added mildly.

With no further word, Sennett and his men left the office.

They swung into their saddles and left the alley. They turned down Main, and then into Stable Street, to bed their horses at the livery. Chitwood was out in the town, the stable boy said; he was frightened and silent as he took their bridles.

They separated at the livery, Beach and Zaragoza heading for the hotel, Sennett setting out to look for Chitwood. Patiently, he tried the poolroom, saloons, gambling rooms. All with negative results. He located him eventually, behind Sennett's own store.

The big September wagon train had come in, with six

59

in consignment for Sennett, and Sennett's competent young manager, Andy Ferguson, was supervising their unloading. Up from the Horn to Frisco, these goods had traveled; by wagon, by twelve-mule hitches, across the Sierra Nevadas, across the fringes of the Great Salt Desert, around the wild Wasatch spine.

The old sense of contentment came over Sennett again for an instant as he watched the muscled wagoners in the lantern light, and the shifting and rolling and canting of crates and barrels and pine packing cases. Steadily the antlike procession of men filled his warehouse; with ammunition, brandies, whiskies; with coffee, kegged candy, corn planters, veneered furniture; with circular saws, bolt goods, tinware. With about everything Cheyenne County could need or desire. Each with its unique distant history of manufacture, all assembled here in flickering lantern light, in a lost corner of the world.

For a moment a feeling of accomplishment came over him again. And then he saw Dewey Chitwood. He was standing with a handful of townsmen, watching the wagons discharge their freight.

He had been in town a year now, and Sennett had never liked him. He was given to plaid suitings and hair salve; his fingers, always dirty, were loaded with showy brass rings. He was hard for Sennett to classify. He had none of the earmarks of a businessman, or even of a gambler. His conversation was larded with the names of all the famous trail-end towns and mining towns, and though he spoke of them with bluster, yet Sennett felt he spoke of them with authority. He certainly knew horses, and he kept a good clean stable.

Now, as Sennett strode toward him, he seemed to crumble.

"It wasn't my fault, Mr. Sennett," he blurted. "You can't hold me responsible."

"It's not in my mind to hold you responsible," said Sennett. He took Chitwood by the elbow and led him beyond earshot of the others, beyond the apron of light, into the darkness. "But I'd like to ask you a few questions."

Here was the public hitching lot, black and empty now. At the south end of the lot was a long, low bench, so placed for the convenience of visiting ranchers and their families. Reluctantly, Chitwood seated himself. Sennett sat beside him, offered him a cigar, struck a light for each of them.

When his cigar was burning to his satisfaction, Sennett said, "All right. Now I want to hear how Jefferson got out of your stall and into Culp Fashner's hands. In case you haven't heard, Culp took him out to Lazy B̶ and shot him. Also, in case you haven't heard, Culp is dead and two of his friends, Morg Morgan and Fletch Parrish, are in jail. How did they work it?"

Chitwood turned to stone. "Look at it one way, maybe I'm responsible after all," he said numbly. "Here's what happened, Mr. Sennett. There was a note on my desk. It said saddle your horse and tie him in that clump of cottonwoods behind the church. Your name was signed to it. I did like it told me."

"That easy, eh?" said Sennett. "Well, I don't hold you to blame."

"That's white of you," Chitwood said. "So I'll tell you something else, something I know and maybe you don't. Culp and them other two never had the learning to write no note." He waited for a moment. "Culp couldn't write," he said. "But his brother Holly can."

"I see," said Sennett. "Do you still have it?"

"No. Old Pete Delaney used it to roll one of them big rollin' pin sized cigarettes he smokes."

Over at the rear of the store the wagons had finished unloading, and had left. Andy Ferguson, alone on the loading platform, was blowing out the lanterns. The arc of light grew smaller and smaller, shrinking at last into spongy night. Overhead, scudding clouds blanked out the moon.

A tendon jerked involuntarily in Sennett's wrist, and jerked again, and he realized he was approaching utter exhaustion. Hatty had started this thing as fit as a fiddle; so had Fashner. But he, Sennett, had been plunged into it beaten and feverish from a long siege of overwork. In his harassment and worry, for no reason at all that he could fathom, Dove's image came into his mind. Came, and altered like vapor, and emerged as the image of Ellen.

"Dewey," he said. "You were there when Buck Needham shot Ellen's father. I wish you'd tell me about it."

"It was just another gunfight, Mr. Sennett. A good man Sawyer Browne, shot by a skunk, this Buck Needham. It was just about early lamplighting. They were in

61

that passage beside my livery stable. Mr. Browne was talking to me and Needham came walking up. They got into a quarrel and Needham beat him to it."

"What were they quarreling about?" asked Sennett.

"Just quarreling."

"But about what?"

This seemed a very natural question to Sennett, but somehow it upset Chitwood. "How's that again?" He sounded flustered.

"Weren't you asked that question at the inquest?"

"No. No, I wasn't. Now let's see. Why, they was quarreling about Hatty, I think. Yes, now it comes to me. About Hatty."

Sennett got to his feet. He was convinced that Chitwood was badly frightened. And why, he wondered, should a man telling the simple truth be frightened? Was he lying? What were Sawyer Browne and his slayer actually quarreling about?

"Good night, Dewey," said Sennett.

Chitwood mumbled good night.

Ordinarily, the arrival of a wagon train would have been of exciting importance to Sennett. Now, as he walked toward his hotel and bed, he tried to recreate the old excitement and anxieties, the mood of costs, prices, discounts. But, strangely, these things now seemed nebulous and unreal.

He had just come out onto Front Street, and was angling cross-corner to Main, when he was slapped with the clamor of bucketing revolver shots.

The inky town was without sign of life. He judged they had come from his left, from perhaps a block away.

He counted them automatically as they whapped and echoed through the deserted night. There were eighteen of them and they came irregularly, almosy lazily, in small bursts, volleys, and singles.

On occasion, in the late hours of the night, some of the boys in the Pastime would get into marksmanship arguments. Behind the Pastime was a vacant lot. Kerosene lamps would be carried out into the weeds and beer bottles would be set up as targets on barrelheads. Unconsciously, he glanced downstreet, toward the rear of the Pastime. The vacant lot was dark.

Not too interested, he crossed the sunken road and climbed the four plank steps to the Main Street sidewalk. He had passed the barbershop, and was approaching the small dark courthouse, when five horsemen pounded out of the alley by his shoulder, nearly riding him down, plummeted down the short grade to the road, and, caroming into each other in frenzied haste, vanished north on Main and into the night.

They had come with a crash and were gone, and almost instantly, it seemed, there was nothing but the still night again, the lonesome clapboard store fronts, and a faint velvety vibration of diminishing hoofbeats, staccato horseshoes against baked earth.

Sennett turned from the sidewalk and strode into the alley. This was a short transverse alley, scarcely forty feet long, connecting with the important lateral of Court Alley behind the courthouse.

Courthouse and jail, facing each other across the alley, were swathed in night and shadow, the dim lamp burning behind the jail office window—nothing at first seemed changed.

Then, in the weak overtones of the lamp, Sennett came to a halt and saw that he was standing in a slaughterhouse.

At his feet, misshapen in death, riddled with bullets—and handcuffed—lay Morgan. Ten feet away, in a trail of blood gouts, was Parrish. In his death spasms, he had almost tied his legs in knots. He, too, was riddled—and handcuffed.

Now, from where he had been leaning against the jail door frame, Sheriff Lytle materialized and advanced upon Sennett. The drunkenness was still on him, and he walked with great care.

He said, "Well, Mr. Sennett, there are your horse thieves." There was the grating of gravel in his voice.

"Back in Alabama," Sennett said softly, "we wouldn't let you guard a henhouse."

When Lytle made no response, Sennett said, "And don't try to tell me these were Anvil men. I saw them. Todd Hatty led them. This is Hatty work. Are you going to tell me that Hatty has suddenly become my champion? They were killed because they were Fashner men."

Lytle said, "I don't know who done it. They didn't speak and they was wearing gingham masks."

"No masks when I saw them."

"That sounds like different fellows."

"Murdered with handcuffs on," Sennett said in repugnance. "Cheyenne County doesn't murder anyone,

63

even horse thieves, handcuffed. What kind of a man are you, anyway?"

Inadvertently, Lytle moved, so that the lamplight from the window touched the side of his face. From hairline to jaw hinge his flesh had been crushed and battered until Sennett doubted if it would ever heal without disfigurement.

Stunned, he said, "You resisted them. They beat you into submission."

"That's right," said Lytle calmly. "No one takes a prisoner from Ben Lytle while he's conscious. There was a minute or two, I guess, when I wasn't rightly conscious. I figured you, or Lazy B, or somebody, would be waiting for them to cross the alley, come morning. So I was taking them across tonight, to hold them in the courthouse cellar until court time tomorrow."

"It wasn't Anvil," said Sennett. "And it wasn't Lazy B. I tell you I got a look at them. It was Todd, and that Curley, with three other Hatty gun-throwers."

"That's what you say, Mr. Sennett. But you ain't exactly unbiased."

"Sheriff," Sennett said quietly. "You're all man. I misjudged you."

"I'm a hell of a man," Sheriff Lytle said bitterly. "But I do the best I can."

# 8

THAT NIGHT Sennett did not sleep in his bedroom, but in the hotel office, on the big black sofa. His experience with Zaragoza some nights previously had shown him the bedroom was far too easy of access. Things were breaking now, and with a vengeance, and he would be no good to anyone, Dove, or Anvil—or Ellen—dead. And you could get just as dead through carelessness as you could through courage. He slept behind a locked and bolted door, against the wall, out of Winchester line from the window, from the rooftops across the street. He slept soundly, and yet tensely, and awakened only half refreshed—and angry.

64

Stripping off his muslin nightgown, he bathed, washing himself with sponge and soap from an ironware bowl, standing in a tin tub kept in the office wardrobe for that purpose. Gradually, his blind anger was supplanted by hunger. He dressed, then strapped on his gunbelt. He wore his gunbelt well about his hipbones and his holster high, rather than low, for he had been trained in the school of deadly marksmanship, and marksmanship almost entirely. He had no faith in a fancy draw. He had seen a good many men killed and ninety-nine per cent of them had been killed by judgment and gunsight, and not by sleight-of-hand.

Bathed, shaved, dressed, and armed, he descended the front stairs into the lobby. Tonight is Dove's garden party, he thought.

Passing through the empty lobby, he entered the dining room and sat down.

As he ate, he had visitors at his table, business associates, coming, sitting an uneasy moment, and leaving. All of them showed alarm and concern for him, but all of them were family men, painstakingly cautious. First came Lew Julian, the hotel manager. Then Charley Shaw and Vince Oakley, his co-partners in the stageline. Finally, Andy Ferguson.

They asked few questions, but gave much information.

The gingham masks had been found in a rain barrel by the Little St. Louis Billiard Palace. The town had been shocked by the outrage, but had vindicated Lytle. Rumor placed the blame variously on Lazy B and Anvil. No one placed the blame on the Hattys, for what could be their motive? All morning, they said, Todd Hatty had been striding up and down Main Street, expressing indignation at Sennett's identification to Lytle, proving an alibi, accusing Sennett himself. It had been very confusing.

Confusing? thought Sennett, sitting alone after they had left. It's as simple as Hatty-style warfare.

Looking at it from Hatty's point of view, what had he gained by it? First of all, he had exterminated two Fashner followers, and so ruthlessly that Fashner himself must have been plenty spooked when he heard about it. For Fashner, you could bet, would have no doubts about the affair. What else? Unexpectedly, at random, Lazy B had been dragged in; but a chastened Lazy B could be a Hatty advantage. Most importantly, however, a vicious slur had been laid against Sennett's reputation.

Yes, from a Hatty point of view it had been a good night's work; all profit, and no loss. But all of them, Oakley, Shaw, Julian, Ferguson—and even Hatty—had missed the point. Actually, Hatty had blundered. As had Fashner.

Two days ago, in the eyes of the county, it had been Hatty and Fashner—with Sennett maligned by each, but bypassed. Then Fashner, by the incident at the old saw-mill, had declared himself against Sennett by an overt act. Now the Hattys had performed the same stupidity.

Through their clumsiness, they had slammed him out of all possible obscurity, beyond recall, into the center of things. From now on, wherever men talked, it would be Hatty and Fashner and Sennett.

He must talk to Dove, Sennett decided. She would be filled with rumor and counter-rumor, distraught and frightened for his welfare. In one way, it was harder on Dove than it was on himself. She must be living in anxiety and panic and concern for him, and unable to do anything about it. On the way to Dove's, he would stop in at Dr. Maddox's. He wanted a word with the physician, and he wanted, too, to pass a cheerful good morning with Hal Durben.

Sennett strolled down Main Street in the midmorning calm and knocked on Dr. Maddox's side door. Dr. Maddox himself answered.

Chunky, grim, he stood in the doorway, the silver rims of his spectacles glinting in the sunlight. He showed neither pleasure nor displeasure at the sight of Sennett.

"Well, what do you want?" he asked brusquely.

"Two things," Sennett said easily. "I'd like to say hello to Hal Durben. Then I'd like a little talk with you."

"With me? With Doctor Maddox, or with Justice Maddox?"

"With Neighbor Maddox."

"Neighbor Maddox is not here," said the physician. "When I came out from Illinois years ago I brought him along, but he couldn't take the beating he got and de-camped. I've never heard from him since. He may be dead, for all I know. But as one solitary man to another, will you permit me to offer you a purely impersonal drink?"

"I will indeed," said Sennett, smiling slowly.

Dr. Maddox turned and Sennett followed him inside, down a dark hall, and into a bright, sun-splashed room. Here were two iron beds, white-painted, each with a tall fan-shaped head. On the bed by the door lay three little Indian boys, convalescing; and on the second, across the room, lay Hal Durben. He was carving small wooden horses from white pine with a kitchen knife. "He's better than medicine for them," said Dr. Maddox. "He makes them toys."

Hal said, "But it ain't the toys they want, it's the knife." Glowering, he added, "I'm feared to give it to 'em. They're three against one."

He repeated the joke in Sioux, and the children grinned happily.

"How's that worthless brother of mine making out?" he asked.

"Fine," said Sennett. "Anything you want?"

"Yes. First choice, Hatty. Second choice, out of this blamed place."

"You'll stay where you are," snapped Dr. Maddox. "And I want no more argument out of you." Addressing Sennett, he said, "Shall we take care of that bit of business now?"

Sennett nodded, and they left the room.

They crossed the hall and came into a cubbyhole which was apparently an office. There were two shuck-bottomed chairs, and a table used as a desk. Its walls lined with bottles and flasks and jars, blue and green and amber, and with tin canisters of herbs and spices. On a short workshelf was a grinding machine, and a mortar and pestle. There was about everything here in the medical line, Sennett reflected, from fruit extracts and candied violets to hog medicine. The trapped air was suffocatingly hot. They seated themselves across the tabletop, and Dr. Maddox produced a quart of whisky.

Carefully, he poured two drinks into foul-looking, chemical-stained glass graduates. They downed them. Despite himself, Sennett grimaced.

"Didn't enjoy it?" Dr. Maddox asked politely.

"Oh, yes. It just surprised me. There seemed to be a faint taste of camphor."

"Alum, in mine," said Dr. Maddox. "Residue from some eye water I mixed. Always variety this way, you see. Going to swear out a warrant against Holly over that horse?"

"I doubt it. I doubt if I could make anything stick against him. I'll probably just talk to him."

"That should be an interesting conversation. By the way, did Anvil kill Morgan and Parrish?"

67

"No."

"Did Lazy B?"

"No."

"I believe you told Lytle it was Todd Hatty and company, but he refuses to credit it. Do you still make this claim?"

"Yes," said Sennett. "But I'm wasting my breath and I know it."

Dr. Maddox said, "Gun and torch, bushwhacking and treachery." His voice was like velvet. "When will this end?"

Sennett made no answer.

"Now you are asking *me* a question," Dr. Maddox said. "You want to know on what ground I stand."

Still Sennett remained silent.

"And I answer you this way, Mr. Sennett. I am a magistrate, and I stand on my oath. By my office I am forbidden the luxury of personal opinion. I will judge, but I will not prejudge. When Hatty is brought into my court, or Fashner, or you, then I will speak."

"Have you a conscience?" Sennett asked.

"I have indeed; a very active one."

"And on what ground does your conscience stand?"

"It stands on decency. In essence, I suspect, it is very little different from yours."

Sennett arose. Twice, absently, he beat his hat against his knee. "Thank you, Doctor," he said.

"Thank me for nothing," Dr. Maddox said curtly. "In time you will become like the others. Already you have killed, and you will do more killing."

"Perhaps," said Sennett.

He walked from the room, down the hall, along the brick walk, to Main Street.

At the end of Plum Street, as he approached it, Dove's big house stood bleak and looming in the merciless heat. The dry channels of last spring's rains still showed their pattern on the grassless yard, giving the place a barren, sterile look. Overhead the sun was white and fiery, an unbearable mirror in a silver incandescent sky. The morning had become a furnace, without motion of air. Sweating at hatband, collar, and armpits, Sennett mounted the steps and knocked. Mrs. Stafford answered his knock and wordlessly, uncordially, stepped back that he might enter. He cast about in his mind for something to say to this

68

spiteful, ambitious woman, and finding nothing at all, said, "Hot."

"My baby's in the kitchen," Mrs. Stafford said. Her mouth puckered. "Busy."

Once more, as he had done many times before, Sennett looked at her and tried to visualize her as a mother-in-law. She was tiny, and poisonous, with a turkey-craw throat and an embarrassing potbelly which, despite her scrawniness, protruded in a little hump of brown taffeta beneath her tight, beaded belt. She seemed scarcely a woman to him, scarcely a human for that matter. She reminded him of something which might have come from a serpent's egg.

Ashamed of his thoughts, and punishing himself deliberately because of them, he said, "The wagons came through from Frisco last night. I have a surprise for you. A bolt of China silk. Your color, lilac."

Lilac was Dove's color; the silk had been for her.

Mrs. Stafford's tallow cheeks showed no feeling whatever. She never refused a present; she never expressed appreciation.

Dove stood at the kitchen table as he entered, preparing for the night's garden party. All around her was the litter of her work, snips of crepe paper, paste, half-finished streamers, scissors; at the moment she was placing candles in paper lanterns. She looked happily distraught, frantically preoccupied, and to Sennett incredibly enchanting. He put his arm about her shoulder. She brushed lightly against him as she moved away, leaving his arm for a moment like a bridge in the air. Instantly, she was in another corner of the room, fussing like fury over a tray of homemade favors. "How much ice do you have?" she asked.

Her eyes were wild, intoxicated. Sennett thought, Now I know the thing that makes her truly happy. Parties. Yet his side tingled where she had touched him, and he remembered her wildness that evening at his hotel.

He answered her question. "Not much. Less than a hundred pounds, I'd say." It was the only ice in the county, buried in sawdust in the hotel cellar, and worth its weight in gold.

"It'll have to do," she said, her voice like a tightened wire. "The problems I have. A hundred pounds of ice. It'll take at least seventy-five for the tub of punch."

"Which leaves twenty or so pounds."

"It pays to always be on the safe side," said Dove. After a moment, she said uncertainly, "John, this is a party for all of our family friends. You understand that, don't you? There might be people present you don't like. Todd Hatty, for instance, will be there. You'll control your temper, won't you?"

"I don't have a temper any more," Sennett said amiably. "All I have left these days is a few ribs, tired muscles, and a battered spinal column. I won't violate your hospitality, if that's what you mean."

On top of the oven was a platter of cookies. Preoccupied, he picked one up, broke it neatly in half, then in quarters, fitted the pieces together, and replaced it. "Dove," he said. "I've come to an important decision."

"Yes."

"I've been living a dishonest life."

She was in the act of snipping crepe paper, and her scissors froze. "With me?" she said a little sharply. "You mean with me?"

"No," he said. "Not with you. I haven't been dishonest with you. I've been dishonest with my men at Anvil."

"Oh," she said in relief. "For goodness' sakes."

He tried to put it into words that would make sense to her. "My men at Anvil are in danger. In double danger, now. From Hatty, and from Fashner. I own that ranch, they work for me, but I neglect them. I give them wages, but that's all I give them. They're entitled to a great deal more. They're entitled to my friendship, and my on-the-spot protection. They're entitled to identify themselves with a boss who at least lives with them. Just think of the taunts they've taken in my behalf, taunts which I never heard about. Dove, I'm moving out to Anvil. I'm making my home there."

"Of course, John," she said. "Some time."

"Not some time. Now."

An invisible shutter seemed to drop between them.

"That's a rather strange place to take a bride," she said. "To a ranch. Punchers are pretty rough. You know what I mean. Pretty coarse."

When he made no answer, she said patiently, "You're not looking at this thing right, John. I can see how, with all the hullabaloo and all, you could get mixed up. But you've got everything turned upside down. I realize, and I think I understand fully, all about the friction between you and Mr. Hatty, but it's not a question of which

70

of you is right and which is wrong. No one could ever settle that. It's just a question of using common sense. Your territory is the town here, Napier. If you just sit steady in the boat you're well on the way to controlling it financially. You're a townsman, and the town is your territory. Leave the range to the ranchers. To Mr. Hatty."

"The town is the range, and the range is the town," said Sennett. "There is no division. And no one should control it. Furthermore, I'm a rancher. That's what I'm talking about. Anvil."

"Anvil," she said. "Hardly bigger than a postage stamp. Try to be logical about this thing, John."

He picked up his hat to leave. She went with him to the kitchen door.

They crossed the back porch, and Sennett descended the three steps to the yard. "John," she said, and he halted.

Delicately, from the top step, her childlike hands patted his lapels and straightened his neckpiece. Unconsciously, his hands rose toward her shoulders and also unconsciously, it seemed, she drifted slightly back, just out of his reach.

"Think about it, John," she said, and gently closed the door.

Aroused and disturbed, he turned down Spring Street and headed for Sheriff Lytle's small house.

# 9

SHERIFF LYTLE'S HOUSE was long, low, and narrow, and painted in two colors, forming two segments; the gray rear segment, jail and office, abutted on the alley, and the house itself, facing Spring Street, was a brilliant blue. Sennett took the short path from the sidewalk and mounted to the tiny porch. Lytle was a bachelor and lived alone. The porch roof was supported by a pair of four-by-fours and at the base of each of these posts, in buckets, ornamental gourds had been planted, their vines running upward on fishlines. From the vines hung the gourds, being variously and artificially shaped by Lytle as they developed. Some were being elongated and strangely

71

curved by cloth bandages, some were growing in tin cans, one was growing in a patent medicine bottle. Strings, rags, rusty cans, and bottles. To passersby on the street, it presented a grubby eyesore.

To Sennett, in an instant of revelation, it seemed the futile, painstaking labor of an unhappy, lonesome fellow human.

As he rapped on the door panel, he decided that he understood Lytle for the first time, and that he was perhaps the only person who truly understood him.

Lytle answered his knock. His injured cheek had been smeared with yellow salve, half melted in the heat, running in trickles down his seamed throat. The bruises and cuts were purple and puffed. Sennett thought, the man's pride refuses to allow him to hide them beneath a dressing; he's even doctored them himself.

Sennett said, "I was just noticing your gourds."

"Admire them?" asked Lytle.

"No."

"Neither do I," said Lytle softly. "But they give me something do in my spare time."

Something independent, something honest, thought Sennett.

He stepped into a dim hall. On either side was an open door, darkened from pulled shades within, bedroom, he guessed, and parlor. Down the hall was the kitchen, where they now went, seating themselves across a table from each other, a big chipped enamel coffeepot between them. Lytle poured two mugs of coffee.

"Sheriff," Sennett said. "I want to ask you a few questions. I can't get that shooting out of my mind. Last night I was talking with Chitwood, and—"

"I don't care to discuss Dewey Chitwood."

"How can you say that when you don't even know how I want to discuss him?"

"I don't want to discuss him any way at all."

"Maybe your refusal tells me something."

"Maybe it was meant to."

"But what?" asked Sennett.

Lytle looked grim and remained silent.

Sennett pondered a moment, reorganized, and came in from an angle. "I believe there was more to Sawyer Browne's death than is common knowledge. I'll put it to you frankly. Could it be that Buck Needham shot him down without warning?"

Last night's whisky had drained from Lytle, leaving him sober but unstrung. He folded his trembling hands on the table. They continued to jiggle. He placed them out of sight in his lap.

"No," he said. "I swear it. Leave this thing alone."

"Buck Needham and Sawyer Browne were quarreling?"

"Right. Chitwood so testified, and I believe it."

"Quarreling about what?"

"About what? About Hatty, I guess. I don't recall the question was asked at the inquest. Everyone felt sorry for Ellen and wanted to get it over in a hurry. Nobody went into details. We all took it for granted that they'd been arguing about Hatty. You got any information to the contrary?"

"No," said Sennett.

Again, there was an interval of tense silence.

Lytle's eyelids, damp and scarlet, clamped together in slots. "You think I'm a Hatty man, don't you, Mr. Sennett?"

"Yes," said Sennett. "Do you deny it?"

"I went to bed a Hatty man, but I woke up a Lytle man."

"I hope it sticks," said Sennett.

"It will," Lytle said mildly. "I been ashamed to look in a mirror. Now, lately, they been piling it on and piling it on until I can't take it." He raised a bony finger and pointed. "Yonder's an example."

Sennett glanced as the finger pointed. Through the kitchen's second door, back through the jail and office, back through the jail door. Beyond the door was the alley, and across the alley, the back door of the courthouse. Here, in a patch of veil-like shade, a man sat in a rocking chair, his hatbrim over his eyes, his legs outstretched, boots crossed at the ankles.

The man was King Damietta, the county bully— Holly Fashner's brother-in-law and personal bodyguard.

"Some days ago," said Lytle, "I swore him in as my deputy. Old Man Hatty made me appoint him, and kept himself clean out of the picture."

Stunned, Sennett said, "I don't understand it. Why is Hatty doing favors for Fashner? Are they in this together?"

"No," said Lytle. "They hate each other. I'm positive. I don't understand it either."

Sennett rose to leave. "Where was he last night?"

"Drunk, he says. But that's no excuse for neglect of duty. I was drunk myself."

"You sure were."

"But I was on hand. Honoring my oath of office."

"You certainly were," said Sennett in quiet respect. "So stop worrying."

Staring at Damietta through the oblong of the door, a dark fury took Sennett. Things were happening with great rapidity, things which baffled him. Slyly and tightly, a hidden web was being woven, enmeshing Cheyenne County and John Sennett in its cunning tendrils. The anger which had been building up in him came to a cold edge.

Lytle, musing, said, "You've asked me a question or two. Now I'll ask you one. Truth is, I'm getting to like you, and I'm going to hate to lose you. Do you honestly think you can whip this thing?"

"Put it this way. I'm damned if this thing is going to whip me."

Impassively, they exchanged glances. "I don't mean to pry," Lytle said tactfully. "But I'm sure as hell curious about your plans. If any."

Sennett said, "Say you're living alone, a homesteader maybe, and you've got a field to fence. A big one. It seems hopeless. You get together your posts and wire, and take a look at them. Now it seems twice as hopeless. But that blasted fence has to go up, doesn't it? What would you do? You'd take off your coat and start at the beginning. That's what I'm going to do right this minute. I'm going to dig post hole number one."

"The way you say post hole sounds mighty like grave," said Lytle. There was a mild rebuke in his voice. "Now I hope you don't break no law."

Unsmiling, without answering, Sennett nodded goodby, and left.

He left through the back door, coming out into the blinding white sunlight of the alley. As he approached Damietta, he said calmly, "All right. Wake up."

Back went Damietta's chair as he stumbled to his feet, startled from his dozing. His lumbering hulk caught its balance and his brutish face twisted and squinted as the fog of sleep cleared from his brain. To Sennett, he had always seemed repulsive and depraved, and now, with the blaze of sun on his scum-coated teeth and flat, cold eyes, he seemed doubly so. Big, crudely muscled, overbearing, there was something fetid about him. He wore one holster, low, and when he recognized Sennett his blubbery hand dropped inconspicuously above his gun-butt. In a hard voice, he said, "Watch yourself, Mr. Sennett. I'm a deputy."

Sennett said, "I know." He hesitated an instant, and said, "That was the idea. I want to make this official. Want to walk to the St. Louis Billiard Palace with me?"

Warily, Damietta asked, "You expecting trouble?"

"Not expecting it, no. But you can never tell."

Sennett could almost read Damietta's sluggish thoughts. This is one play, whatever it is, he was thinking, that I'd better be in on.

Unctuously, he said, "Well, come along. And remember, the law don't show no favorites."

And that, thought Sennett, is a warning if I ever heard one.

Side by side, they walked to Main Street.

The Billiard Palace, run by Blackie Faquier, was a Fashner hangout, as the Pastime was a Hatty hangout. It stood alone, between a small tanyard and a lumber yard, and its cheap pine front had been crudely painted to represent brick. One leaf of its swinging doors had been torn playfully in the past by the nine-slug shot of a man-loaded shotgun. It was a part of Main Street particularly avoided by women, who crossed the street rather than pass it. Here the wooden sidewalk was about eight inches or so above the road level. Directly before its door was a huge iron caldron, the largest Sennett had ever seen, always full of water and used as a public watering trough. On either flank of the caldron was a hitching rack. It was this rack that Sennett inspected as he advanced, for here, almost always, could be found a Fashner mount, or a mount somehow connected with the Fashner clan. Four horses stood here, wilted beneath the hammer blows of the sun. When his gaze reached the end of the line, he could hardly believe his luck.

His gaze rested on a giant mouse-colored animal, strong-loined, with powerful chest and thighs. It was Montefrio, one of Holly's top horses, and Sennett knew it well, from nose to the Tumbling F brand. He knew the saddle, too. It was Fashner's horse, loaned to Damietta. It was wearing Damietta's saddle.

His glance passed carelessly over Montefrio, and returned to Damietta.

"We could use a witness or two," Sennett said casually. "Got any friends hereabouts?"

Perplexed, but interested, Damietta raised his voice and yelled, "Blackie!"

Three men came out of the saloon; Blackie Faquier, a hard-looking, swarthy little man, and two half-blood vaqueros. They formed a tight, mean-looking little knot in the doorway, and waited.

Sennett inspected them, one by one, with perfectly blank eyes, and said, "I have a little business to transact, but first I'd better tell you about my state of mind. I'm a man that minds his own business, and you know it. Ordinarily, when I'm pushed, I step aside. Not much, maybe, but a little. But things have been pushing me a little too far. I've seen my friends shot before my eyes, and have had other friends, good decent men, badly beaten. At first I tried to step aside, but my stomach couldn't take it. I've had hardly a meal a day for the last five days and hardly four hours' sleep on an average night. I'm in a bad way."

Damietta grinned, but Blackie Faquier, more astute, frowned and waited.

"So what?" asked Damietta.

"This is what I'm getting at," Sennett said reasonably. "When I'm doing the right thing, as I see it, as I'm doing now, I don't much care what happens. I don't care whether I live a month, or a week, or three minutes. I thought it was only fair that I explain it to you."

There was a strained silence.

"Thank you," said Blackie. "I believe you, and thank you kindly. I'll step back inside. I heard about you and Johnny Flint."

To Damietta, Sennett said, "What's your saddle doing on my horse?" He pointed at Montefrio. "Take it off."

Nervously, Damietta said, "That's Holly's horse and every man in the county durn well knows it." Emboldened, he added, "You take him from that rail without a bill of sale and you'll wish you hadn't. Cheyenne County don't have much patience with horse thieves."

Sennett let that pass. "I don't need a bill of sale," he said. "This isn't a sale. It's a swap. By rights I should take the saddle, too. Do you want it, or don't you?"

Emotionlessly, Blackie warned, "You're looking at your coffin, King. You better do what he tells you, and pronto."

Like a man of clay, Damietta clumped to Montefrio.

The roll of bulbous flesh at the base of his neck glistened in sweat. He loosened the cinches and dropped his saddle to the dust.

Reins in his hand, Sennett led the horse around the rack, up onto the boardwalk. It followed him docilely, a sleek, beautiful giant. Noon traders were circulating in and out of the shops now, and over and over he was forced to weave Montefrio through clustered gossipers. They gaped, but he ignored them.

Repeatedly, in a soft but clear voice, he said, "You've got a new name now, horse. Jefferson. Steady there, Jefferson. Come along there, Jefferson, old boy."

That afternoon Sennett spent at his store, with Ferguson, and at the stage office, with Shaw and Oakley, catching up with his business affairs. The town was somnolent under the heat, and the slow, sticky hours passed without event. During the afternoon, too, he had sent to the Stafford home the ice from the hotel and, from the store, half a case each of canned peaches, pears, and blackberries, for the punch.

At a quarter of eight, in the office of his store, he put on a new shirt and cravat, and tried to get himself mentally set for the prospect of a dull but obligatory evening. He put his gun and gunbelt in the office safe; it was not intrinsically valuable but it was precious to him sentimentally and he wanted no petty pilferer walking off with it.

The rule tonight would be "no decorations." During his residence in Napier, Sennett had been to many other such social affairs and he knew that this rule was strictly and conscientiously obeyed. No sidearms meant no sidearms. Enemies gathered with enemies, and attempted to conduct themselves with at least a modicum of decorum. At times, of course, this had worn pretty thin. He had seen, at such social functions as this, belt-buckle whippings, cannings, and blizzards of fists—but always away from the ladies, behind some outbuilding—and never a gun. Even the sight of a gun was impolite.

Blue, satiny night was on the town now, peaceful and still. First, as he approached, he saw Dove's party as a powdering of golden light in the darkness, and heard it as a murmur of voices; then, as he came to the end of Spring Street, and entered the yard, he was engulfed by it. Things were in full swing.

Just about everyone of importance or pretension, financial or social, was there, town and county. Sennett's quick eye calculated, appraised, sorted. Todd was on hand, freshly shaven and sporting a lawyer-type black suit and string tie. He had a julep in his hand and, loudly, with convolutions of his lips and shattering horselaughs, was attempting to blast himself into a focal point of attention and admiration. Old Man Hatty was absent. Ellen was absent, as was all of Lazy B. Fashner was absent too; he would be, Sennett thought, he couldn't make the Stafford grade.

There were no trees in the Stafford yard, so the crepepaper streamers and Chinese lanterns looped from poles driven into the hard, baked earth. From the back porch an organ wheezed out cultured Eastern airs and somewhere in the crowd, to Sennett's left, Mr. Stafford—who had never been farther east than Pawnee Fork—was experimenting with a Boston accent. The elite of the county was cautiously, and a little stiltedly, feeling its social oats.

Dove was everywhere, enchanting in lilac tulle. Twice she flew past Sennett, touching him with a brushing of warm, intimate fingertips, in a sort of a secret, affectionate communication—touching him, and vanishing.

He looked around him. People answered his restrained salutations, even talked to him a little, but were much too precise in their courtesy. In five days, he thought dryly, he had become a dangerous stranger to them.

A plank table had been set up by the porch steps. On it were plates of withered sandwiches, dead insects killed by the lamp, and the big tub of punch. Elbow-deep in acquaintances and yet alone, Sennett sampled the punch. Its surface floated with mangled peaches, pears, and blackberries, a tepid mess despite his chunk of ice which bobbed in the fruity scum. He blew out his breath, vibrating his lips with impatience and disgust, and sought out Dove. He had already paid his respects to Mamma and Papa Stafford, and had been deftly edged into the sidelines.

Well, after all, he thought, I'm not marrying Mamma and Papa.

Dove was moving through the crowd, serving cake. He located her by her voice. Todd Hatty was across the yard, standing spread-legged and bent-kneed, talking in a bellow to a group of townsmen. He was expressing opinions and laying down the law on about every subject that came into his head. And Dove, as she moved here and there through the crowd, kept adding words and phrases to Todd's sentences. She made it sound as if she and Todd were having a private conversation.

When Sennett finally cornered her, she asked, "Are you having a good time?"

"Wonderful," Sennett said. "Wonderful."

Suddenly, magically, Todd Hatty loomed up beside them. His coarse face was red in the lanternlight, and his big chin was cupped inward, hugged into his collar. He's looking for trouble, Sennett thought; if it's a little safe trouble, and not too much.

In heavy sarcasm, Todd said, "Do my eyes deceive me? Why, it's Sheriff Sennett. The Alabama sheriff that carries his badge in his pocket."

Sternly, Dove said, "Now I don't want you two boys fussing."

"Where did you hear about that badge?" Sennett asked.

"Nestor was telling Ellen Browne, and Ellen told my old man."

Lovely, sweet Ellen, Sennett thought. Getting things twisted again.

"Said it was so old it was rusty," Todd went on. "Know what I think? I figure you tote it around and flash it when you get in a hole, hopin' it might scare somebody."

Modulating his voice with infinite care, Sennett said, "As I've already explained, that badge belonged to my father. I also carry my mother's locket. Would you care to slur that up with your dirty tongue, too? If you would, you'll never get a better chance."

"John," said Dove, shocked. "You promised me."

Gently, Sennett said, "Listen, kitten. Go away. This isn't for you."

At the outer edge of the front yard, by the street, a welcoming pole had been erected with three barn lanterns swinging from it. These lanterns cast a circle of greenish-yellow light on the hard, parched earth. Now, into this illumination, stepped four men. Hatty punchers. They stood for an instant, silent. They wore dusty range clothes, and their faces showed suppressed excitement. Throughout the yard, conversation stilled, as though it had been severed by a saber slash.

Suddenly, in the tomblike interval, the Chinese lanterns on their wires seemed tawdry and the crepe-paper foolish.

79

One of the punchers said, "Is Doc Maddox here? Lytle has just been killed."

Sennett pushed forward. "How?" he asked. "And by whom?"

"Shot. Five times. By Old Man Hatty."

"Doc Maddox is out to Little Wagonspoke setting a broken jaw," someone yelled.

Now Dove's guests had gathered about the punchers, and questions flew.

The story came out in a hurry. It had happened in the alley by the barbershop. Lytle had been leaning against the door, and Old Man Hatty had walked by, and Lytle had abused him under his breath. Naturally, Old Man Hatty had shot him. That was all there was to it. Hatty had then gone directly to the sheriff's office, as any decent law-abiding citizen should, and had given himself into the custody of Deputy King Damietta. When deputy, now sheriff, Damietta heard all the details and listened to three witnesses, Hatty riders, he had released Mr. Hatty and complimented him on his courage and sense of honor. A slight crowd had gathered in the sheriff's office by then, and Damietta had explained to everyone that Lytle had overstepped himself and exceeded his authority.

In Sennett's mind, things began to clarify. He remembered how Johnny Flint had tried to goad Lytle to his death, and how Lytle had avoided it. Very apparently, Hatty had sensed the prospect of Lytle's defection from him. So he had appointed a new sheriff—in his own manner.

King Damietta would be a good Hatty sheriff. He was ambitious, brutal, and had no scruples. The evil was intensifying. When Old Man Hatty, unprovoked, Sennett knew, had burned those five cartridges he had made his power absolute.

Dove stood alone, to one side. Her fingers were fanned, pressed deep into her cheeks.

Coming up beside her, Sennett said, "Now I have no choice. Now they need me at Anvil more than ever." Soothingly, he added, "But this is no time to talk about it. Good night, kitten."

And what, he wondered as he returned to his hotel, was the situation now? Now truly, without license, Hatty was the valley's lord and master. One by one, Sennett considered the persons involved and how they were affected by the night's doings.

If things had been critical for Sennett before, now they were unbearable. Any gun seeking him out from a darkened doorway could have Hatty law behind it; even now, as he walked the shadows of Main Street, he was living and breathing under whim, under Hatty whim.

Ellen Browne—how was she affected? Hatty had offered her the hand of spurious friendship; now that hand was filled with invisible gun steel. Completely now, though he might choose to conceal it temporarily, Lazy B was in his grasp. With Lytle's death, and with Damietta's ascendancy, Hatty was Ellen Browne's true ruler.

How did Fashner stand? Fashner, Sennett reflected bleakly, was a dead man. Damietta had sold him down the river, and Holly Fashner, certainly, and above all others, would be Hatty's most pressing job. He would be hunted, slyly, warily, mercilessly, from east to west, from valley floor to foothill, night and day. He had gambled, his card had turned, and he had lost.

A picture came into Sennett's mind of the county, with its grasslands and gullies and distant rocky verges, of small cabins and lonely, isolated ranch houses. Groups of men rode, shabbily clothed, but on fine mounts and with fine guns. They rode the valley crisscross, up and down, and no child or woman or man could evade them. They would nest in one great warren, and that warren would be the Hatty ranch house. And they would not be marauders or assassins. They would be posses. Carnivores duly and legally authorized, deputized by Damietta.

Lamps were low in the lobby of the Napier House, and the place seemed deserted when Sennett entered. To the left of the stairs was a door which led to the manager's quarters. As Sennett rested his boot on the first stair, the door opened. Lew Julian, sleepy-eyed, with a frockcoat thrown on over his naked torso, said, "One of your Anvil hands, Willie Durben, is at the Emerald Isle with a message for you."

Sennett withdrew his foot from the step and was on his way to the front door when Julian said, "Something else. Miss Ellen is spending the night here. The way I get it from her, she came to town to consult you. She's up in Seven and wants me to let her know when you get in."

Sennett hesitated. "I'll see Miss Ellen first." He turned and started for the sitting room. "Would you bring her down, Lew?"

"Sure," Julian said expressionlessly. "You bet, John."

The ladies' sitting room was, as usual, almost unendurably stuffy. For an instant Sennett stood in the dark by the little table and its lamp, a match poised but unlit in his hand. In that instant he saw Ellen Browne as he had never seen her in actuality: honest and clean, profoundly brave, and, somehow, incredibly beautiful. It was an Ellen Browne that came to him almost in a dream formed from a hundred tiny memories to live before him now, unnerving him, standing so close to him in imagination that he could almost feel her presence.

His hand unsteady despite himself, he struck flaming match to lampwick and refitted the glass chimney in its brackets. The room came at him in the light, with its odor of sachet left by unnumbered women guests, with its scent of dry carpet. With the flush of light, Ellen vanished and another phantom, Dove, appeared.

Perspiration—from worry, from tension, from the layered heat itself, moistened his eye and he wiped his face blankly with his coat sleeve. For an instant again, Dove was in his arms, against the background of gaudy wallpaper. Now mentally, as before physically, he disengaged himself from her.

Slowly, the image of Dove, too, vanished.

He was in the midst of a weary grimace when Ellen came into the room. She drifted in arrow-straight and drowsy, freshly awakened, and seated herself fastidiously on the edge of a chair. She was wearing a slightly mussed navy blue dress with perky white starched cuffs and collár. She had come to town, Setnnett knew, in a divided riding skirt, but like all ranch girls, had got out of it in a hurry and into more feminine garb. Apparently she had been napping in the dress, waiting for his return. Napier was a remarkable town, he reflected. A sheriff could be shot down on Main Street, yet a few blocks away no one seemed to notice.

He stood for a moment, drinking her in. The fog of sleep still hung about her and as she smiled at him, slowly, unguardedly, it was like lightning to him. The crash of a thought came to him, and he wondered if it were possible for him to be in love with both Dove and Ellen.

It was obvious that she had something important to tell him. Gravely, sleepily, she tried to organize it in her mind, it seemed, tried to present it to him properly.

Finally, she said, "Mr. Sennett, I'm having trouble with my riders."

"Oh, I don't think so," Sennett said negligently. "I'm sure there's nothing to be alarmed about. Everyone is a little rattled these days." His calmness steadied her instantly. Now what? he wondered. What in the hell now? This could be bad. It was a new Ellen before him now, slightly frightened, less assured.

"I don't know why it's you I've come to," she said stiffly. "If you're surprised at it, so am I."

"Let's hear about these riders who are causing you trouble," Sennett said. "You mean Ed Nestor too?"

"Ed's the only exception. He says to sit steady. The others are restless. He's trying to find the shells and return them to me. I'm telling you this in confidence, of course."

Sennett raised an eyebrow. "Shells?"

"My father had bought eight cases of Winchester ammunition to be used, I'm ashamed to say, against Mr. Hatty if the time should ever arise. We kept them locked in a little room in one of the barns. The hasp has been pried from the door and the cases are gone."

"So you have thieves at Lazy B."

"There are no thieves at Lazy B. Not one. When you realize that, you will realize how serious this is and why I'm frightened. Those shells were taken by honest men. Lazy B men took Lazy B ammunition to use in the interests of Lazy B. At least I'm sure that's the way they're looking at it."

"I see," said Sennett.

The worst of it, the point she had missed, was that she had lost her grip, that even Nestor had lost his grip. This, Sennett thought bleakly, could be the forerunner of real disaster. No ranch can be bossed from its bunkhouse. And if they took them so freely, they would use them twice as freely.

Quietly, Sennett asked, "Who are they preparing to shoot at? Anybody in particular? Or just shoot?"

"They're seething at Fashner."

"Who isn't?" Sennett said. He frowned. "But here's the real difficulty. Say you got a cache of Winchester shells. You keep thinking about them. You don't want them to corrode from disuse, do you? Shells mean power. Soon you're in the mood to pop them at anybody." Hesitating an instant, he asked, "You don't think they turned them over to Hatty? Not that Hatty needs them."

"I know they didn't. I hate to admit it, but about half of my men appear to distrust Mr. Hatty a little."

83

"So it boils down to this. Lazy B, without permission of owner or foreman, is hitting the warpath?"

"It's pretty awful, isn't it?"

"It certainly is. For if they go at it blind, they don't stand a chance. Things have changed considerably in Cheyenne County in the last hour."

He told her about Lytle's death, and about the new sheriff.

She refused to believe that Lytle's shooting was intentional. Why would Mr. Hatty want to kill such an ineffectual sheriff as Lytle, and why would he want Damietta, Fashner's brother-in-law, to become sheriff? Sennett realized that this is what the town would think, that Damietta was a Fashner man and that Lytle had probably held Fashner sympathies.

He shrugged, then said, "Mr. Hatty has a plan. And a Lazy B on its high horse isn't according to this plan. Today they may be against Fashner, but tomorrow, you see, they may be against Mr. Hatty himself."

"Oh, no. Never. Never against Mr. Hatty."

He gazed at her mildly, no longer bothering to argue Hatty with her. Such bullheaded, badly misplaced loyalty was almost inconceivable to him.

"Here's the situation," she said. "All my hands trust you. You mind your own business, and so far, it seems, you've been minding it pretty well. Little by little, you've been building up something of a reputation. I won't say it's the kind of reputation that I find charming, but that's beside the point. You're popular out at Lazy B. Even Ed Nestor gives a satisfied sort of grunt when your name is mentioned. I wonder if you would come out and talk to my men and try to quiet them."

When he remained silent, considering, she said humbly, "Please don't make me ask you again. I couldn't say those words again."

"You're overrating me," Sennett said. "But I'll come." He paused a moment, calculating time, estimating the danger point, and added, "In a few days."

Then he told her he was moving to Anvil. She looked relieved and pleased.

Sweeping her skirts with the palm of her hand, she arose. "Good night, John," she said. "I won't even try to thank you. I'll just say good night."

"Good night," said Sennett.

Standing there, she seemed suddenly hazy, lost, submerged almost hypnotically in a world beyond reality. The contagion spread to Sennett, and she became unbearably magnetic to him. He fought the pressure driving him to her, and conquered it, half turning his back on her, and thrust his numb hands listlessly into his coat pockets.

To say something, anything, speaking over his shoulder, he said, "Buck Needham—the man who killed your father. I can't get him out of my mind."

That broke the spell which had come over them. But it was a cruel way to do it.

Completely self-possessed now, completely matter of fact, she said, "What about him?"

"Well, for one thing, where did he go when he left? I know he fled the county, everyone says so, but where did he go? Have you ever heard?"

"We had a drifter working for us once who said he'd heard in a roundabout way that Buck Needham was in Buttonville."

"Buttonville?"

"It's a sort of town."

"The way you say it, it sounds like Hades."

"As I understand it, they both have the same mayor," she said. "Good night."

As she moved to depart, he said, "Wait," and then, "Nothing," as she turned to him.

He turned down the lamp, blew out the flame, and together they left the sitting room, walking into the lobby.

Old Man Hatty was in the lobby.

He was standing by the stairway, his thin shoulder blades leaning against the newel post, superficially presenting a picture of grubby dejection. From dirty black broadcloth to lumpy, misshapen boots, he gave off a spurious aura of misery. As Sennett and Ellen approached him, he pinched his sly, withered face into an unhappy frown and said humbly, "Miss Ellen, I come here to see you. I'm troubled about what I had to do tonight, shooting Lytle and all. This old heart of mine won't leave me have no ease until you let me explain."

In that way—before Sennett even opened his mouth—he got in the first shot.

Nervously, Ellen said, "But why explain to me, Mr. Hatty?"

Ignoring Sennett completely, Hatty said, "Because to

me you're just like my little daughter growed up. I love you, and I want to stand high in your opinion."

"You do," said Ellen tensely. "You do, Mr. Hatty."

Sennett glanced at Ellen. She was staring at the old man and her belief in his essential innocence was so profound that her face was wretched in sympathy for him.

"We're getting sidetracked," Sennett said. "Let's hear that explanation."

Gruffly, Hatty said, "It wasn't for you, it was for her. But it ain't private. Well, here it is. I kilt Lytle, just as they said. He was by the barbershop door, and I was passing by. He called me some bad names and I shot him. Any decent man would have done what I done, but that ain't what bothers me."

"Now that's something we'd like to hear," said Sennett. "What *does* bother you?"

"Stop sayin' we. I'm not talking to you, I'm talking to her. Here's what I'm tryin' to say. Lytle was once a close friend of mine. I didn't shoot him just because he called me those names, though that would've been reason enough. I kilt him because I knew the meanness that he was planning. The hurt he was calculating for the county. He give off that he was a honest human but he had sold out. He had sold out to Holly Fashner."

Well, thought Sennett grimly. Here's a liar that's really a liar.

"How horrible," exclaimed Ellen.

"It sure was, daughter—if I can call you daughter." The old man screwed up his face piteously. "Look what the times and that Holly Fashner has brought me to. Forcing me to shoot an old friend for the good of the county. But I won't get no credit for it. All I'll get is blame and sneers and ugly rumors."

Once more, Sennett looked at the girl. She was completely in the old man's spell. If she had believed him innocent before, now she believed him not only innocent but a martyr.

"But to them that low-rates me," said Old Man Hatty, "I got an answer."

"That also we'd like to hear," said Sennett.

"It's this. How could I possibly profit from Lytle's decease? No way at all. He was a Fashner man, true, and I removed him, true, but what about the new sheriff? What about Damietta? He don't profit me none either. Why, he's Holly Fashner's brother-in-law."

86

"So," said Sennett sourly, "according to your reasoning, you're worse off than you were before."

"That's it. And there's your proof that my intentions is purely honorable."

"You don't have to prove anything to me," said Ellen tenderly. "And you know it."

"Thank you, daughter," said Old Man Hatty. Tremulously, he held his hat across his chest and gave a little bow.

They watched him leave.

When they were again alone, Ellen said, "There goes a wonderful old man. A kind-hearted man, if only people understood."

"But you understand him," said Sennett.

"Yes."

"No," said Sennett. "But he certainly understands you."

Leaving her by the newel post, he went out onto the street. The evening's excitement had disappeared and Napier slept. He retrieved his gun from the safe at his store, then headed for the Emerald Isle and Willie Durben.

# 10

JUST about every town has its best and worst neighborhoods. Napier's worst was small, but plenty tough. It lay just out of town, a scant quarter mile to the south, and was called Popskull for its high grade of whisky. It consisted of half a dozen shanties, two rooming houses for drunken punchers, one brothel, and two one-room saloons. The smallest of these saloons, and the dirtiest, was the Emerald Isle. The old military road was Popskull's main street, and its physical division from Napier was a broad creek bed, dry throughout the year but for the brief spring floods. As Sennett, walking in the night, came up the road from Napier, he crossed the log bridge over the creek bed, its dead weeds and potholes of rubbish silvered in the moonlight, and came into the center of the silent, clustered buildings.

The shabby, inky structures crowded a crossroads. There was only one light; cater-cornered from where Sennett stood, an oversized lamp hung from a beam over the door of Lola's Millinery Shop, the brothel. Its wash of white light was globelike and limited, touching only the shopfront and a disc of the rutted road before it. To Sennett's left, almost indistinguishable in the darkness, was a low, small hulk which was the Emerald Isle. Its single window had been obliterated with black carriage paint and no whisper of light showed, but there would be activity within, he knew.

He knew, too, that he might be unwelcome here, for the Emerald Isle's clientele was small but exclusive. He tried the doorknob, found the door locked as he expected, and knocked.

A crack of light showed, scarcely the breadth of a thumb, and a deep Irish voice said amiably, "We ain't open for business."

"Willie Durben," Sennett said, and the door closed.

Almost before he knew it Willie was standing in the shadows beside him. He'd come out the back way. The Emerald Isle certainly didn't take any chances.

Under his breath, Durben said, "Mr. Finnegan said to offer his apologies. Fact is, he's strengthening up a batch of rye with his own secret formula of cayenne, tobacco, and a wonderful powerful-looking green powder he keeps hid in an old shoe, and he don't want no strangers around. Let's find some place and sit down."

Two rickety chairs, cushioned with ancient folded quilts, stood at the side of the saloon, facing south. They seated themselves. Shadows were like ebony here, and across the corner Lola's guiding lamp seemed a hundred miles away. The conversation at first was formal and casual. Willie had come in for a dual purpose, he said; to bring a message to Sennett and to visit his brother Hal at the doctor's. Hal, he was glad to discover, was mending well. How had things been going with Sennett?

This sort of talk was good to Sennett's ears. Good old Alabama country-style talk. Courteous, preparatory, saving the point until last.

After a bit, Sennett said, "I was just talking with Miss Ellen Browne."

"That's nice," Durben said.

Sennett shot him a quick hard look in the dark.

"Yes," said Sennett, a little flustered. "Yes. Miss Ellen tells me now it's Lazy B. From what she says they're all dressed up and ready to go."

"Against who?"

"They say Fashner, but you know how it is. It could be Hatty or—with the wrong kind of spark—even against each other."

"Or even Anvil, with the wrong kind of spark. We're setting out there next to them. Mr. Sennett, this county's hell, ain't it?"

"Yes. But it's got some mighty good cows and some mighty good grass."

"And some mighty good people, if you just take time out and really look for 'em. Oh, I'll own they're pretty well hid at the moment, but they're here."

Sennett snorted.

Silence grew around them. Finally, Sennett asked, "What's this message for me, and who is it from?"

"It's from Beach. He wants the key to the closet."

The closet was in the parlor of the empty Anvil ranch house. There was nothing in it but a few cases of ammunition and a half dozen or so carbines.

Sennett said slowly, "So Anvil, too, wants to get all dressed up and ready to go?"

"That's about it," said Durben. From his voice you could tell that he agreed with Beach. Tonelessly, he said, "He's having trouble with his men. They know now Flint killed Trego on Hatty's orders, so they're making war talk against Hatty. They break out in a froth at how Culp Fashner shot Jefferson. They're making war talk against Fashner."

"Well, at least they're ambitious," Sennett said dourly. In his mind he ticked them off: Beach, Zaragoza, Wallace, Durben, McCrae. Five indignant, outraged men against a horde. The idea was so hopeless that it chilled him with pride.

Switching the subject, he asked, "Willie, did you ever hear of a place called Buttonville?"

There was a dull pause and Durben's voice, when it came, sounded startled. "Why, no," he said. "Why, yes, maybe. What about it?"

"Buck Needham's there. I want to talk to him. How far is it?"

"Two days' hard ride, as I get it, and I mean hard. Stay away from Buttonville. It's a no-good outlaw hangout, deep in the mountains, and I don't figure it'll cherish a visitor."

"Can you find it?"

"Me? I don't know. Maybe."

"I want to leave in about an hour, traveling fast, with light rations. Will you come along?"

"Looks like I'll have to."

Across the road from them, down a little, there was movement. That was the way they first noticed it, as a shifting of shadow.

The lantern before Lola's Millinery Shop hung motionless in the still air, lighting the gray, blistered shop front, the log doorstep, and a patch of the rutted, sun-hardened military road. Up this road, from the south, as yet beyond the touch of the lantern, came a solitary horseman, walking his mount. But it was not this horseman who had attracted their attention.

The shifting shadow had come from the side of the building and now, as they watched, three men emerged from Lola's side door. One by one they materialized, flattening themselves against the clapboards. A few feet from the road, around the corner from the approaching horseman. The horseman came on.

Sennett got to his feet, slipping his Colt from its holster. Abruptly, he felt Durben's fingers on his wrist, fingers warning him to check himself, to wait and see.

The horseman came into the pool of light. It was Holly Fashner, on a wiry gray horse. He rode stiff and straight in the saddle, suspicious, alert. He's lived that way for days, Sennett decided, hammered between greed and terror. His rifle, clasped at trigger and gunlock, was held upright at his hip. His coarse, vicious face had lost its bluster and showed the ravages of ceaseless fear. He must be coming into town to square things with Damietta.

Pistol shots rolled out, riding each other in their concussion, drumming the night. Waist-high, by the shadows along the building, gunflashes burned golden and copper red in the pounding clamor. Fashner wilted from his saddle, lifeless, and mounded himself grotesquely on the earth. The little gray, riderless, cantered into the darkness.

Now the shadows by the building advanced into the lantern light and became men. Their leader, his long auburn ringlets fluffing out from the back of his hat, wore black batwing chaps.

This man, with the toe of his boot, turned Fashner over, examined him, and was satisfied. Contemptuously, with the edge of his bootsole, he scuffed dust into the dead man's face.

Quickly, with his companions, he vanished into the night.

"Now I do believe I seen them batwing chaps before," murmured Durben.

"This is just the beginning," Sennett said. His voice grated a little as he added, "I've changed my mind. I'm going to give Beach his key. I'll have it sent out to him."

Round about them, as they moved to depart, the buildings remained dark, silent. Popskull was no stranger to bellowing guns. It listened, but it stayed indoors.

Within the hour, according to schedule, Sennett and Durben were on their way to Buttonville.

At the hotel, Sennett had left the key with Julian, to be delivered to Beach, and in the hotel kitchen they had stowed a few light rations in their saddlebags. Sennett's big watch said six minutes of one as they trotted their mounts past the last of Napier's scattered houses, onto the valley floor.

Stars hung low above them, and the endless sky was as deep purple and as bodiless as port wine. They bore northeast, toward the as yet invisible mountains. They limited themselves only to the endurance of their horses and the severity of the trip ahead of them. The time element, Sennett reckoned, was going to be highly critical.

Dawn came, and the encircling mountains appeared with it, multicolored, far-lying, graven in startling clarity. Noon passed, with a little rest, food, and water. Then it was dusk. The mountains were rushing at them now, sending out fingers of scrub from their foothills to meet them. Just after sunset, in the slate-gray of early night, they passed a knot of ghostly cattle. "Maybe we better cut a little south," said Durben. "Them's Hatty cows."

Sennett nodded, and veered. "You know, Willie," he said. "They look just about like any other cows, don't they?"

"Not to me, they don't," Durben said. "They look mean, and sneaky, and slobberin' for other folks' grass."

Night was well upon them and, always climbing, they had shuttled their way into the foothills, when Durben said, "Here."

In the moonglow, Sennett saw the great mountain buttresses rising above him. Directly ahead, a fan of alluvial gravel spread down between two gigantic, wind-polished boulders.

They walked their horses up the apron, turned left at Durben's word, then right, and were in a slanting scene of trees once whipped by some forgotten tornado, fallen and rotting, each nested with huge, ancient roots, up-thrusting and knuckled and spidery. Beyond the trees began the true ascent.

It was the roughest climbing that Sennett had ever done. Intermittently, and constantly, it seemed impossible. After a bit, he set himself but one goal. To keep contact with Durben.

At midnight, Durben said, "We'll eat," and they dismounted.

Where they were, or how far they had penetrated, Sennett hadn't the slightest idea. He knew only they had not yet reached the crest.

They ate sitting on their heels, on a tiny patch of leafmold, almost beneath their mounts' bellies. They allowed themselves a little water, too, and a smoke. As they smoked, Sennett's mind wandered back to Napier, brooding darkly. "You see what Hatty's done, don't you?" he said at last. "By two quick killings, Lytle and Fashner, he's raised his own man, Damietta, to sheriff and probably taken over the South Association, too. Now he has no organized opposition at all. Now he controls the entire county."

"He don't control me," Durben said softly.

"Nor me," said Sennett.

# 11

BEFORE dawn they crossed the ridge, buffeted by a lashing, razor-edged wind, and began their descent. The exhausting climb had badly punished Sennett, but Durben appeared unchanged. He had looked tired a month ago, sitting on a bench; he looked tired now, to exactly the same degree. Sennett had the sensation that earthly things —gales, rocks, brush—existed in their own special world and Durben, frail, eternal, in his own. At midmorning they ate again, beside an icy stream. There were giant trees here, and the forest floor was mottled with shadow. The heat increased as they descended. During the entire journey there had actually been little talk between them, Sennett wondering how Durben could know so well the path he was following with such unwavering decision, Durben withdrawn behind those crystal-blue eyes, absorbed only in the horses and the trail.

Once he gave a signal, and they pulled into a ravine. Three horsemen passed, mounted on incredibly beautiful mares and leading pack mules. They were gaunt and cruel-faced, in misfit odds and ends of clothing, arrogant and viper-eyed. They bristled with weapons and were very drunk. One of them wore a beaded vest much too large for him, with a patch of dried blood about the size of a saucer where someone else's heart had once been.

When they had gone on, Durben said, "South country men, I'd say from their stirrups. And a billion miles from home, if they ever had a home, bless their plunderin' hearts."

"Now how could you tell all that by just looking at them?" Sennett asked, letting marvel creep into his voice.

Durben lapsed into a tight silence.

The slope became less steep, but more matted with foliage, and, abruptly, about two hours before sunset, the trail led them out upon a rocky ledge strewn with giant egg-shaped stones. The path continued downward at an angle now, through a split in the shelf. They tethered their horses and walked to the edge of the escarpment.

Here the mountains formed a small enclosure, and at first Sennett could see nothing below him but almost sheer broken outcroppings and the green intermingling billow of treetops. Finally, patiently adjusting his vision, he saw a small dog. And dogs meant humans.

"We're right over the village of Buttonville," said Durben. "It's below us, on this side, hid by an overhang. The going from here on looks hard, but it's easy. You'll be there before you know it. But not, by golly, before they know it. That's why they got them dogs." He studied Sennett through half-closed eyelids, and asked wryly, "Do you think you can find a saloon."

Sennett grinned.

Durben said, "All right then. Find that one down there."

From his saddlebag, he took a heavy object wrapped in a blue bandana; he unfolded the cloth to reveal a rusty ax head.

"First thing when you get down there, make for the saloon and ask for Palmer, the owner. Give him this ax head, tell him you want to sell it, and ask him to name you a price. Then you and him will be the best friends in the world, maybe."

Sennett took the ax head from Durben's hand.

"Ax heads, you know," said Durben, "usually run from three to four and a half pounds. Five-pounders can be got but they ain't ordinary. This is a five-pounder. It'll tell Palmer you're recommended. I'd like to come along with you, but that wouldn't make things no easier for you. Who knows, maybe I wouldn't be popular down there? If you ain't back here by daylight, though, I might take a little pasear just for a look."

"If I'm not back by daylight," Sennett said, "cut for home."

Making no answer whatever, Durben led his horse into the scrub, and Sennett began the final descent.

As Durben had said, the lower path was good. The slope was gentle and the footing sound. The scrub became denser and the air dank and loamy as Sennett neared the valley floor. All at once an unseen battery of dogs began to bark, and his horse flinched at the yelping hullabaloo. Then he rounded a boulder to find himself at the bottom, in Buttonville.

Beyond a small meadow and a stream rose stubby cliffs topped by ascending terraces of jumbled rock and trees. Close at hand, to his left, the cliff was widely undercut, and in the shelter of the overhang was a scattering of hovels; some were log-and-sod cabins, others were scrap lumber shacks, apparently from packing boxes, wind-proofed with sheets of old tarred canvas. Midway along their line was a larger, sprawling building, drab, unpainted, with a long hitching-rack. The place seemed deserted.

The pack of mongrels snarled about him as he dismounted and unhitched. He wondered how many rifles pointed at him, and just how he looked in the notch of a gunsight. Pushing open the saloon door, he entered a dim, mouldy room.

Here, too, there was no one in sight.

The room was large, walled and floored with rough pine. From the rafters hung a homemade chandelier, fashioned with candles and tomato-can reflectors. At the rear was a second door, open, and a man appeared in the doorway.

He was brawny, bald, and stripped to the waist. Hair swirled on his meaty chest and along the tops of his arms like black smoke. He carried no weapon.

Sennett asked, "Mr. Palmer?"

The man yawned and nodded.

"I want to sell an ax head," said Sennett, and produced the blue bandana. Palmer took it from his hand and said, "Step back here."

Sennett followed him into the back room.

This room was a small store. With a professional eye, Sennett appraised it. Though small, it was heavily stocked with staples. Mr. Palmer apparently did much business with gentlemen who traveled far and fast on the barest essentials. Carefully, Palmer laid the ax head on scales and weighed it.

"Five pounds," said Sennett.

"So I see," said Palmer.

Sennett said, "I want to see a man named Buck Needham."

"But does he want to see you?" said Palmer, hefting the ax head. "There's the question."

"Why not ask him?"

"Mebbe I'll do just that."

Beyond the doorway, men straggled into the big front room of the saloon, four or five of them, dusty and travelworn. One by one, as they came into view through the doorway, they inspected Sennett with cold eyes. Leaving Sennett, Palmer joined them. Sennett watched him lighting candles, moving leisurely about, setting out bottles and glasses.

Outside, twilight had fallen. Napier, like the Tombigbee Swamp, seemed a shadowy memory, far away. A wave of exhaustion came over Sennett and despite himself he dozed. Half awake, he found himself thinking of Ellen Browne, and also of his childhood.

Palmer had rejoined him now, and was standing before him, inspecting him placidly.

"I didn't catch your name," said Palmer.

"I didn't give it."

"Of course," said Palmer.

From beneath the counter he produced a gunbelt, and buckled it about his naked waist.

"Afraid of bears?" asked Sennett.

"I'm afraid of you," Palmer said calmly. "Let's go."

A short passage behind the little store brought them

95

to the rear of the building, and out into the open. Swift night had come, filling the mountain pocket with soft, impenetrable ebony. Palmer grunted, and wheeled left, and Sennett followed. "Here," said Palmer, and stopped, and Sennett's outstretched fingers touched the rough logs of a cabin.

Palmer unlatched a slab door, and they entered.

Outside, as he had touched the cabin wall, Sennett had given a quick look about him in the darkness. The cliffs, like black broken teeth against a tiny star-studded sky, the meadow, the filmy huts, were almost nonexistent in the swath of night. The only light stood out before Palmer's saloon.

And it was this picture that came back to him now, the picture before the saloon. He again saw the five horses tied at the hitching-rail, weary, heads hanging, powdered with candle shine. A gray horse, a buskskin, two blacks, and a calico.

Sennett's roan was missing.

Palmer said, "You got a visitor, Buck. He come recommended."

The cabin was earth-floored, foul, without windows. There was neither stove nor fireplace, but a circle of ashes in the middle of the floor and a smoke hole in the roof. From a hook on the wall hung a rancid ham hock. A chunky cowboy sat at a crude table, curing snakeskin in the light of a strip of rag burning in a cup of grease. He had a square, doughy face and oily, tangled hair. He disliked Sennett on sight, and showed it. In a leaden voice, he asked, "Well, what do you want?"

"I see this is going to be private," said Palmer, "so I'll be getting along."

Needham said, "Stick around. I may have call for you. I don't much care for this. I never laid eyes on this rooster before."

"Okay," said Palmer carelessly. "Yes, okay." He scarcely moved, but his gun was in his hand, negligently.

"You can believe me or not," said Sennett. "First I want you to get that straight. It's up to you."

"Well, thanks," said Needham. "Thanks."

"Say Old Man Hatty sent me. Would that make sense?"

"It would," said Needham. His big knuckles were clenched and white, carefully motionless on the table-top.

"Say he paid you a certain sum to kill Sawyer Browne and then moved you out of the county, here to Buttonville. Maybe now he's prepared to pay you a little more if you move on a little farther, down to Mexico perhaps. Does that make sense, too?"

"No," said Needham.

For an instant, Sennett was flabbergasted. His reasoning must have been completely false. Quickly he tabulated the facts as he knew them, and tried to come up with something logical. He came up with a baffling vacuum.

Indolently, Needham asked, "Would you like to hear what really happened?"

He was primed to talk, so Sennett simply waited.

"First," said Needham, "I'll put your own words right back on you. You can believe me or not. It's up to you."

"I have a feeling I'm going to believe you."

"All right." Needham nodded. "Here's the way it was. It was in the late afternoon. I was in the Pastime Saloon. Old Man Hatty drifted in and sent me around to the Napier Livery Stable to pay a small bill for him. He was kind of excited, yet I didn't think nothing of it at the time. So I went. Well, like I say, it was coming on night, and Sawyer Browne was in that passage by the stable, gabbing with Chitwood, the owner. Browne had a cigar in his mouth and was just striking a light. He didn't speak to me, and I didn't speak to him."

"Then what started the quarrel?"

"There wasn't any quarrel. Somebody called Mr. Browne's name and we all turned. Todd Hatty was standing in the office, just inside the open window, in the dusk. He shot Browne three times and Browne fell. Then Todd climbed over the sill to us, yanked Browne's Colt out of its holster, threw it onto the ground, and said to me, 'You shot him in a fair fight, Buck. Chitwood here will swear to it.' Then Todd walked away."

Needham went on. "About half an hour later I run into Old Man Hatty and three of his meanest riders. 'Get out of the county,' they said, 'and now.' I seen they meant it and sure did. Know what I think?"

"Haven't the slightest idea," said Sennett. "But I'm mighty interested."

"I think Hatty figures now he made a mistake in letting me go. As long as I live, I might stand up in court and swear a rope around Todd's neck. Then Todd would swear one around his papa's. Now Old Man Hatty can't have that, so he sent one of his gunslingers to wipe me out."

"That's something I hadn't heard about," said Sennett.

"Well, you're hearing about it now. I'm talking about you."

This was a bad moment. Even Palmer was becoming restless.

As though he were speaking to a thickheaded child, Sennett said quietly, "If I were a Hatty man, he would have sent me here with a good idea of the true story, wouldn't he? Or at least with a story that you could listen to and that wouldn't give me away as I gave myself away. If I were a Hatty man I wouldn't come here accusing you to your face of Browne's killing, would I? Both of us would know it was nonsense. I came for information, and I got it."

"He's right, Buck," said Palmer.

Needham said, "Are you a law officer?"

"No."

"I didn't kill Browne; Hatty never paid me a penny, not even my back pay, and he run me off without even a blanket."

"Thanks," said Sennett. "I'll be moving along. That's all I want to know."

"But that ain't all we want to know," said Palmer. "Are you crazy, messing around with me this way? Who are you? Who gave you that ax head?"

A soft Alabama drawl from the doorway said, "I give it to him." Durben, his rifle aslant in the crook of his skinny arm, blinked in the guttering, smoky light.

"Why, it's Willie Durben," said Palmer, faltering. "The Alabama Cottonmouth."

"Don't call me that," said Durben gently. "I've told you before, time and time again." To Sennett, he said, "If you're ready, we'll start. We got a long, hard trip."

Out of the cabin, in the darkness beyond the threshold, Durben broke into a lope and Sennett followed him. Sennett had entered the pocket from the west; now, as they ran, they moved north. They had waded the stream and were crossing the meadow when a faint shouting sounded in the distance and Sennett turned his head. Before the saloon, a crimson torch streaked the black night and men mounted in haste. The hunt was on. He and Durben rounded a fallen shaft of stone, and here, tethered by Durben's pony, was Sennett's roan. Dryly, Durben said,

98

"I stole your horse for you. This place can be easier to get into than to get out of. We'll head north, then circle back west and lose 'em. The long way is the short way tonight."

They began a slow climb up a creek bed, dense foliage interlaced above their heads.

In the cobalt and pewter of pre-dawn, they breakfasted near the crest, along a tongue of rock over a misty chasm. When they had eaten, Sennett said, "Willie, it wasn't a fair fight after all. Sawyer Browne was ambushed." Gravely, omitting no detail, Sennett recounted the story.

Durben listened, poker-faced.

"Todd Hatty was the one that did the killing," said Sennett. He paused, and added, "Dewey Chitwood saw it. Chitwood's been lying."

Unhappily, almost inaudibly, Durben said, "I pity Miss Ellen."

"I pity Todd Hatty," Sennett said coldly.

They stared into the misty vapors below them. The sun was rising, striking the crags to clotted vermilion, burning through the mists in luminous gold.

Very carefully, Sennett said, "Now don't go off half-cocked. Here's something I must ask you. I don't expect it, but there may come a time when you'll need me to stand beside you, so I ought to know what's what. How do you know about Buttonville? How is it that Palmer seems so intimate with you. Are you and Hal outlaws?"

"No."

"Then I don't understand it."

"We ain't outlaws now," said Durben, amused. "But we was." His voice took on a note of stern reproach. "There's a great deal of difference between is and was, John."

"There certainly is," said Sennett, giving a soundless laugh. "There certainly is. You remember what you told me once? Well, I tell you right back. You're a man I can never repay."

Later, they slept, and it was noon when they again took the trail. The mountains about them were chaotic and confusing and, to Sennett, completely strange. But Durben knew them very well. Toward the middle of the afternoon, Sennett realized they were following the ridge of a spur, and abruptly the trees cleared and they saw their valley beneath them. It lay like a great green and brown saucer, sweltering in the thin air. Far across the valley floor, against the amethyst haze of the distant uplands, Sennett could see a few dazzling flecks of white. Napier. They faced the short axis of the valley, and far to Sennett's left, against a blue-glass sky, were the two raspberry smudges of his Big and Little Anvil. The Hatty ranch house lay well to his right, behind a shouldering cliff, out of sight.

Directly below them stretched the land of the late Knutson—Hatty-killed—land now untenanted. Crowding it, well within view, was Hatty range. The Hatty boundary at this point was the old military road, now the stage road. Just down the slope the road curved, and there was the building known as Stop Six, a horse change for the stageline. It stood on Knutson land and faced Hatty land across the road. It was frequented at times by Hatty riders, but now, as they appraised it from above, they saw no ponies either at its rail or at its rear. They descended the slope and approached it.

Stop Six, dusty in the heat, had a main building, sheds, and a good stable. Its main building, sun-scorched and unpainted, was part residence, part hostel.

Sennett and Durben stepped into a large, cool dining room. Against one wall was a homemade showcase displaying tobacco, rock candy, smelling salts, commodities for travelers, and cartridges. Down the center of the room was a long table. The proprietor, a gangling, lachrymose man in patched workclothes, was at the table, reading an old newspaper by holding a pair of spectacles over it, reading-glass fashion. He greeted his guests warmly, and they shook hands. Without a word, he went to his kitchen and returned with cold roast chicken, a cold beef roast, cornbread, honey, a tureen of rice pudding, and a pitcher of thick, chilled cream.

As they ate, Sennett said, "We've been away. Anything happen, Mr. Burgess?"

"No, sir. Not a thing."

Absently, Sennett looked at the spectacles on the table. The nosepiece had been broken some time in the past and ineptly soldered. One earpiece had been lost and replaced with a hook of fencewire.

These were McCrae's spectacles. In Sennett's mind they were as much a part of the old ranch cook as his faded green plush cap. He rarely wore them in public but carried them in his big wallet, wrapped in butcher's paper, for emergency use. He treasured them above all things.

"Where did you get those spectacles?" Sennett's voice had iron in it.

"From a Hatty rider," said Mr. Burgess. "From a fellow knowed as Curley. He sold 'em to me for a dime."

"When?"

"Why, this morning. Anything wrong?"

McCrae, a recluse, never left the ranch. They would have to kill him to get them.

Sennett kicked back his chair and stood up. To Durben, he said, "They've raided the ranch. We've got to get to Anvil."

# 12

I was early morning when they reached Anvil, crossing Knutson land, skirting Lazy B, going southeast, then south. Twice during the night Durben's weary pony floundered; even Sennett's fine roan labored. It was a hard, sickening night, but the morning brought worse.

They could see the devastation as they approached. When they arrived and dismounted, it was unbelievable.

The ranch house had been half burned, then dynamited. Barns, sheds, bunkhouse, stood charred and gutted, or strewn and splintered like crazy jackstraws. The well had been dynamited. It had been a methodical, malevolent job. Nothing existed but the white-hot sunlight, the black, ugly embers, the great fire-scarred cottonwood, and, high in the dazzling tinfoil sky, three tiny black dots, weaving and gliding. Three buzzards.

Durben was looking, not at the ghastly wreckage, but at Sennett.

Sennett's bronzed cheeks were stiff, his eyes, behind their dust-caked lids, thoughtful and remote. He was looking at the great tree which had once stood not far from a doorstep.

"I know trees, Willie," he said. "I was raised in a swamp, with trees. It's been badly burned, but it will live."

Tartly, Durben asked, "And what does that mean?"

"It will mean a great deal," said Sennett in a matter-of-fact voice, "when we rebuild. A good ranch house should have a good tree in its yard."

Durben listen numbly. He's out of his wits, he thought.

Raising his voice, Sennett called, "Beach! Hilario!"

There was no answer.

A long, heartbreaking search of the wreckage gave them no information whatever. Everywhere were pitiful reminders—clothes, kitchen utensils, fire-blued bits of metal and fire-eaten leather, but no true answer to the catastrophe. It was Durben who made the first discovery.

When Trego had been shot by Johnny Flint, he had been buried beneath a neat mound, out behind one of the barns. The barns were rubble now, and Durben, having searched their wreckage and passed beyond, came to Trego's grave. He let out a call, and Sennett joined him.

Behind Trego's grave was a second grave, so new and fresh that its earth was a raw, brown wound.

"McCrae," said Sennett dully. "Whatever happened, there are Anvil men alive. And they have buried McCrae."

It was while they were standing by the graves, their heads uncovered, that Beach came to them. A few yards away rose the slope of Little Anvil crag, and Beach came down the mountainside, scrabbling, falling, sliding, breaking his descent by clutching saplings and outcroppings.

It was a Beach they hardly recognized, earth-smeared, glassy-eyed, and, for a moment, breathless and mute with rage and depletion.

He drew a long breath, held it deep in his lungs, and released it slowly. "Well, they did it to you, John," he said. "We turned out useless after all. They wanted to do it to you, and they did."

"Not to me," said Sennett quietly. "To you. And they'll pay for it."

"Hello, Tom," Durben said mildly. "I don't generally recommend baths, but you sure as hell could use one."

"Tell me about it," said Sennett.

Beach said, "Not here. Follow me."

He scrambled up the steep slope, through the thick brush and jagged rock, and they struggled after him.

High up the slope, they came to the lean-to. It was constructed of new-cut branches against a boulder and before it Zaragoza squatted in the moss, cleaning two small trout. He was as dirty as Beach, or dirtier, and his face as he worked, before his eyes met theirs, was shockingly savage and merciless. When Sennett spoke to him and he raised his head his face relaxed. He asked, "Are you all right, John?" and when Sennett nodded, he said, "We buried McCrae." When Sennett made no response, he said, "McCrae was my mother and father."

His hands moved clumsily as he cleaned the trout and Sennett noticed that they were blistered.

Beach said, "Hilario pulled him out. He'd been long dead, of course."

"Wallace is missing," Sennett said. "Where is Wallace?"

Beach opened the lean-to by the simple process of tossing aside an armful of branches. Wallace lay, half sitting, half reclining, his back supported by the boulder. He had been shot through the shoulder, and was picking out wisps of dry moss which had been applied to the gaping wound to staunch the blood flow. Sennett, who knew gunshot wounds, realized he was in a pretty bad way. When Wallace saw Sennett, he smiled in genuine pleasure and asked, "You all right, John?"

"Stop asking me that," Sennett said curtly. "Of course I'm all right. What are you all trying to do? Humiliate me?"

"You know better than that," Beach said.

Equally, Durben said, "He don't mean no harm, boys. He's had a rough four days."

Changing the subject, Sennett said, "Now I want to hear about it."

Beach told it, talking slowly, painstakingly, pausing in recollection to omit no detail. The others listened with motionless faces. The assault on the ranch had come yesterday morning, just before dawn, and from the beginning it was obvious that the intent had been utter annihilation and massacre.

McCrae had saved them, and by accident. He had started his breakfast duties in the cookshed and gone out at dawn toward the barn, to break an egg in the mouth of a sick calf. Halfway to the barn, four men had loomed up before him in the gloom. They were strangers. He had wheeled, dashed to the bunkhouse, shouted the news, and started at a stiff-legged run for the big house to warn Zaragoza; in these days of emergency Zaragoza had been sleeping in the parlor at Beach's orders. Three other men were crouched by the big house's kitchen, firing the building at its foundation. Again McCrae yelled, and Zaragoza came dashing out into the night, piling over the veranda railing.

"That's seven," said Sennett.

"We figure they was about sixteen, all told," said Beach, and continued. One of the men at the kitchen porch, the one with the tinder, was Todd Hatty.

Beach himself saw him for, in the meantime, Beach and Wallace, snatching clothes and weapons, had rushed from the bunkhouse. The haystack was in flames now, and one of the barns. To Beach it had seemed that there were Hatty men everywhere. In the red-gold light of the burning barn, in the center of the ranchyard, stood McCrae. He was the center of a triangle formed by three small groups of ravage-hungry killers, probably ten yards from the nearest. He was alone, unarmed—for he was a man of peace and ordinarily as gentle as a baby—and highlighted by roaring flames which showed even the horn buttons on his ragged vest. Just an instant he stood there, but in that instant he raised an old, knobby finger, shook it indignantly in the air, and shouted, "You git home, all of you. I never seen such goings-on. Git home."

Then the volley hit him. Beach reckoned at least twenty bullets.

"All they wanted was for us to make a stand," said Beach, concluding, "so we cleared out. We couldn't do nobody no good dead, so we moved. We'd figured out before to meet here if we had to, so we did. I guess that's about all. Wallace picked up some lead somewhere while we was moving and maybe I slapped one fellow down with my Colt, but I wouldn't swear to it."

Zaragoza, it developed under Sennett's questioning, had recognized Old Man Hatty and, to his surprise, several of the old Fashner group. Wallace had seen the Hatty gunslinger, Curley.

"Didn't they try to hunt you down?" Sennett asked.

"As a matter of fact they did," said Beach, "but it didn't really come to anything. They made several attempts to dislodge the Anvil men from the mountainside, but were pretty easily discouraged."

"What about the dynamiting?"

"They hung around until dawn, burning and dynamiting. They took with them all horses, too, probably to be loosed in the foothills."

"What about McCrae's burial?"

Beach and Zaragoza had come down the slope in midmorning and taken care of that. McCrae's body had been thrown into the smouldering wreckage of the big house. Zaragoza had pulled him out. Then they'd gone uphill again, to doctor Wallace, and to wait for Sennett and Durben.

Sultry-faced, Beach said, "Blast it, I ain't sure what I'm going to do about all this."

"Naturally," said Durben.

"What do you mean, naturally?" asked Beach.

"Because it ain't your choice," said Durben. "You ain't the boss."

Unoffended but interested, Beach said, "Now is that so? Well, if I ain't the boss, who is?"

Durben said, "John Sennett's the boss, or ain't you heard?"

"Oh," said Beach. "I see what you mean. John understands what I'm talking about. He's the Napier boss, I'm the Anvil boss."

Idly, Sennett said, "Sorry, Tom. I've always been the Anvil boss. I guess I just didn't show it."

"You're going to show it now?"

"Yeah."

They stared at him with a mixture of pride and doubt and downright uneasiness.

Pondering a moment, Beach said, "I surely don't mean to pry, but what are you going to do? What are your plans?"

"Well," said Sennett in mock gravity, "they say Canada is a fine, law-abiding country. I've gathered together a pretty nice stake. I thought we could all slip away some dark night, and start from scratch up in Canada."

Wallace shut his eyes and gritted his teeth. Durben's jaw hung down, slack and angry and stupefied. Zaragoza looked swiftly and mortally injured.

Beach was not fooled. Beach laughed, satisfied.

"He jokes?" Zaragoza asked, hopefully.

"He jokes," said Beach.

"The Hattys are savages," Sennett said, his voice void of feeling. "Very well, then, here are my plans. I'm going to educate them."

It took them a moment to assimilate it. Then the tension began to slip away. Only Durben commented.

He said, "That just saves me tacklin' it alone."

"No one's going to tackle anything alone," Sennett said. "I want you to get that straight. Now I'm going

105

to give some orders." He revolved his glance slowly about the grim, haggard circle. "First we get some sleep. About midnight I want you to wake me, and I'll head in to Napier. There's a Napier end to this business, and I'll have to handle that myself. I should get to town about noon. In the meantime, Willie's pony, too, will be getting a little rest.

"Just before daylight, Durben will take Wallace to Lazy B, leave him to be cared for, borrow three good mounts, a fresh one for himself, and a little food, and return here. Then the three of you, Beach, Willie, and Hilario, will go to the Knutson ranch house and wait for me."

Beach said, "But the Knutson place is empty. It's been empty ever since Knutson was murdered in his barn."

"Yes," said Sennett. "I'll meet you there tomorrow. And keep an eye peeled."

"This ain't exactly what I had in mind," Beach said.

"I think it is," said Sennett.

Beach nodded, and left them, scrambling down the mountainside to take care of the roan and pony. Sennett only hoped his roan would get him in to Napier; he had little doubt of it, really, for the roan could recover quickly.

Durben was asleep. Sennett lay on the ground, rolled on his stomach, pillowing his face in the sweaty broadcloth of his folded arms, and was out like a light.

Zaragoza wakened him at midnight. The mountain sky was blue-black and the air against his cheek was like frost. Groping and stumbling, he made his way down the slope and mounted his roan. He was in his saddle, and a good five miles on his way before the fog of slumber cleared fully from his brain. He rode slowly, steadily, with no effort at concealment, and reached the fringes of the town without incident when the sun was at its zenith.

At a gentle trot, he entered Main Street, and turned into Stable Street. Following his own advice to Beach, he kept an eye peeled, for he was convinced that the time had come when Hatty would shoot him on sight; Hatty, and probably the Fashner crowd, too. Napier, burning under the noonday sun, seemed a ghost town.

The clumsy building which was the livery, sere and gray in the blasting heat, showed no sign of life. The passageway which flanked it was empty.

Dismounting, he left his roan in this passageway and went on into the yard beyond, the beaten earth quadrangle enclosed by the stable itself, and by three sides of dilapidated sheds. In the center of the yard, near the well with its wagon-wheel windlass and the watering trough, was Dewey Chitwood and one of his stablemen. When they saw Sennett walking leisurely toward them, their eyes protruded, but neither of them spoke.

Turning his reins over to the stableman, Sennett said, "Give him a good rest. Fix him up."

The stableman stared at the roan. "We sure will. He looks like he's earned it."

"He has," Sennett said shortly.

When the stableman had left them alone, Chitwood said ingratiatingly, "This is mighty fine of you, Mr. Sennett. Keeping your business with me after I let Jefferson get away from me that way. I know it wasn't my fault, and you know it wasn't my fault, but a lot of gentlemen wouldn't be so forgiving about it. I ain't seen you around for a few days. How are things out at Anvil?"

Chitwood was a Hatty man; Chitwood was in Hatty pay. Buttonville had proved that. Very possibly Napier hadn't yet heard the story of the wrecking of the ranch, but the grapevine wouldn't keep silent forever. A Hatty rider, drunk, would make a slip; or a drifter, passing through, would bring the word. Possibly Napier hadn't heard it, but certainly Chitwood had.

And the longer it remained unreported, the easier it would be for Sheriff Damietta to whitewash it.

Chitwood's remark told Sennett two other things, too. It told him that Hatty had no idea that Sennett had gone to Buttonville, and also that in the confusion of the raid Hatty had assumed Sennett had been present but had escaped with the others.

Well, Sennett thought, let's give Hatty both barrels. "I passed through Anvil just yesterday," he said. "The rest of the time I was out of the county."

Chitwood barely concealed his surprise. "Out of the county, you say? Now I hope you had a pleasant trip. Maybe you went to talk to the railroad people about that track they're fixing to lay?"

"No," said Sennett. "I went looking for a place called Buttonville."

Dewey Chitwood turned from man to sagging, bloodless meat. When he spoke, though, his voice was careless, under perfect control. "Buttonville? Why, that's that outlaw hangout. Did you find it?"

"No," said Sennett. "It must be pretty well hidden. I'll give it another try, when I'm not so busy."

Chitwood came to life again. His face calmed itself. His body became revitalized, almost swaggeringly so. "Why were you looking for a no-good place like that?"

"Buck Needham's there. He wants to sell me some information."

"Information? What information?"

Sennett looked completely at a loss. "You know as much about it as I do."

As Sennett turned to leave, Chitwood said, "And you come home by way of Anvil, eh? How are all the boys?"

Afraid to look Chitwood in the eyes, afraid the rawness of his soul would give him away, Sennett said evenly, "The boys are gone."

"Gone?"

"And McCrae is dead."

"Why, I never heard the like!" exclaimed Chitwood. "You mean they killed that nice old man then high-tailed?"

"Some time within the past few days," Sennett said, "Hatty raided the place. He killed McCrae, drove off my men, and burned and dynamited."

"I can't believe it," Chitwood said angrily. "I can't hardly believe Hatty would allow such a thing." After a moment, he added, "Could it have been Lazy B, do you think? No, if you say so, but I don't scarcely see how you could be sure. What are you going to do?"

"It was Hatty, all right," said Sennett, "and it's just a question of time before he hunts me down. I guess my days are numbered."

Chitwood looked gloomy.

In a low voice, Sennett said, "Would you do me a favor, Dewey?"

"Yes, indeed!"

"Can I swear you to secrecy?"

"You bet, Mr. Sennett. I've been on your side all along. You surely ain't got no doubts about that?"

"No. Well, here's the situation. Maybe Beach and Zaragoza, and the others, haven't left the country. Maybe they've just scattered into the mountains. Maybe they'll come drifting into town, to your stable, asking for me."

"I get it. What shall I tell them?"

"Tell them I'm in hiding. Out at the old Knutson house."

"Pretty smart," said Chitwood, beaming. "Nobody would ever look for you there. That place has been deserted for months. Yes, sir. I'll tell them."

"And tell no one else."

"No one else."

Grinning, sweating, Chitwood stood in ·the sunlight watching Sennett leave. He looked like a man who had just won a fabulous stake at poker. His fat thumbs were hooked into the armholes of his vest and his grimy, beringed fingers fluttered like predatory butterflies.

Sennett gave him a parting glance, and the sight. nauseated him. He had no doubt that Hatty would get the story, and quick. And that, after all, was the most important thing.

# 13

THERE were two ways from Chitwood's stable to Dr. Maddox's. The first was along Main Street, past the business district. The second was out of the back gate of the stable yard, across a vacant lot to Spring, and thence, through a second vacant lot, to Maddox's back door. The second was shorter and safer, and time was at a premium.

He was halfway down Spring Street when he approached the house of ex-Sheriff Lytle, deceased, and Sheriff King Damietta, incumbent.

There it stood, back a little from the sidewalk, low and long, painted, as Lytle had carefully painted· it, blue in front, gray for the jail at the rear. Somehow it seemed a different house to Sennett now, sneaky, and a little loathsome. He was about to pass its walk when he noticed the porch. The porch was bare. The network of gourd vines, with its rags and strings and tin cans, had been cleared away. To anyone else, Sennett reflected, to anyone not knowing the circumstances, the sight was an improvement; to Sennett, those vines represented the refuge of an honest, baited man, the last sanctuary of a man's conscience. Their absence added to the accumulation of the general hell of his mind, brought him to an unreasoning, simmering boil.

Completely on impulse, hardly aware of his action, he turned into the walk, mounted to the porch, and, without knocking, entered the front door.

From his position just within the threshold, he could see down the dim hall into the empty kitchen, and into the jail office at the rear, also empty. Close at hand, on left and right, were bedroom and parlor doors, both shut.

Twisting the knob of the bedroom door, he opened it and stepped inside. The sleazy window shades had been pulled against the battering of the outside sun and the room was murky in a half-light. In the gray gloom, he could see a human rat's nest. Whisky bottles lay on the floor with cigar butts and soiled clothes. On the bed, on a mattress without bedclothes, lay King Damietta, sleeping off a drunk with mutterings and grimaces. He was wearing an undersized blue-and-white striped muslin nightgown which scarely reached his enormous hams. That nightgown had been Lytle's; Sennett himself had sold it to Lytle, at the store.

Walking across the room, Sennett stood beside the bed. How long he stood there, staring at the creature, he was never sure. Perhaps fifteen minutes, perhaps three.

Almost from the impact of Sennett's will, it seemed, Damietta waked.

The muscles of his eyelids lifted slowly, but the spark of intelligence in his eyes waked instantly, with a flick. In a sandy whisper, he said, "John Sennett. What do you want?"

"Think back," Sennett said. "How many men have you killed?"

"Me? Why, nobody. Nobody at all. Never."

"I wish I could say the same," said Sennett.

Damietta recoiled. Fright flowed into panic, panic into hysteria.

Remote, brooding, Sennett said, "Stop squirming. Answer these questions. Just yes or no will do. And the truth. Do you understand?"

"Yes, sir."

"Do you know that Anvil's been raided?"

Damietta grimaced and shook his head.

"Has Holly Fashner's riffraff thrown in with Hatty?"

"Yes."

"You're doing very well," said Sennett. "Now, Lazy B.

Are there any Hatty men working undercover for Miss Ellen at Lazy B?"

"Yes. No— I mean, not yet."

There Hatty had slipped, Sennett thought. Just one Hatty man in the Lazy B bunkhouse and it would have been the end.

This was the big one. This was the information Sennett really needed. "Is my name on the Hatty list? Are my days numbered?"

Damietta nodded, terror in his face.

"Just one question more," said Sennett. "A personal one. Do you actually believe that any one man—Hatty, for instance—can bullwhip the whole county into subjection? Do you believe that he will rule Anvil, and Lazy B, and every other ranch, from one end of the valley to the other?"

Damietta mumbled, the muted words scarcely intelligible: "He rules 'em already."

With no comment, Sennett left the room and the house.

Outside, he strode a few feet down the walk, cut abruptly back through a vacant lot to the Maddoxes' and knocked on the physician's side door. Mrs. Maddox let him in. She was one of Sennett's favorites, who had seen everything from scattergun artistry to ax work, and never lost her dumpy, fussy, angelic poise. The worst desperado, with an ounce of lead in him, was no different to her healing hands than a baby with colic. At the moment, there was a dusting of flour on her triple chin and a smear of cake icing around her mouth where she had been tasting her own concoction. She gave him a deep, warm appraisal and said, "Come in, Mr. Sennett. It's good to see you're alive."

He stepped inside. "It's good to be alive," he said affably. "Did you think I was dead?"

Without answering him, she led him down the hall and into Dr. Maddox's office. The stocky little physician sat at his worktable, baize sleeve protectors over his shirt cuffs, surrounded by his flasks and bottles and jars. He was even more somber than usual, and his lips were drawn and strained. When he saw Sennett, he said accusingly, "Explain yourself, sir. If it's not you in that grave, then who is it?"

Startled, Sennett said, "What grave?"

The story had finally come to town, and Dr. Maddox had heard it within the last few minutes at the Pastime.

A floater, off trail, had passed the wreckage which was Anvil and had brought in the word. He had seen the two graves, the old one which was Trego's, and the new one. Napier's rumor had placed Sennett in this new grave.

Sennett said, "There's a better man than me under that mound. McCrae."

They waited for details, for further explanation, but he gave none.

Mrs. Maddox said, "How long since you've had a meal?"

"Yesterday morning, I think," said Sennett. "There are more important things than food."

"Hah," said Mrs. Maddox, outraged. "Sit yourself at that table, young man."

Sennett slumped into a chair across from the doctor, and Mrs. Maddox left the room. "I haven't time for this," Sennett said. "I'm in a hurry."

"You're always in a hurry," said Dr. Maddox. Sardonically, he added, "This might be a bad time for you to collapse. Do like the lady tells you. Eat."

"I've got to be moving. I'll eat on the way."

"You'll eat here. With knife and fork, from plate and table. It's better for the digestive juices."

Obliquely, Sennett asked, "That little black mare of yours, the one with the three white stockings. Is she gunshy?"

"I bought her from a cavalry officer over at Fort Riggs. Does that answer your question?"

"Yes. Can I borrow her? Or better yet, will you sell her to me?"

"I'll give her to you. Free. On one condition. Tell me what in the hell happened at Anvil."

"Hatty, plus some Fashner dregs, raided us."

"That's not a very full answer, but I guess I'll have to accept it."

"I guess you will." Then he asked, "Has Hal Durben heard about this?"

"Unfortunately he caught it when I told Mrs. Maddox."

"What did he do?"

"Went to sleep."

Incredulously, Sennett said, "Went to sleep? That doesn't sound like Hal."

Dr. Maddox's eyes twinkled. It was the first time that Sennett had ever seen the doctor truly enjoy anything.

He said, "Well, not at first, exactly. When Hal first heard it he piled out of bed and began ranting and yelling for guns and knives. He thought you'd been killed, and seems to like you. So I gave him a little laudanum, and he went to sleep."

Their eyes met, and they grinned.

Through the doorway, from the direction of the kitchen, came the banging of pots and pans. The smell of frying steaks and sputtering eggs seeped in to them, the ethereal fragrance of hot biscuits and the intoxicating scent of hot coffee.

"I'm a little hungry myself," said Dr. Maddox in appreciation. "I haven't had my dinner yet."

He paused for a moment, and then said, "The most important thing of all, the purpose of your visit, hasn't been mentioned. Why?"

"Because I'm going to ask you to do me a favor—I'm going to ask you to risk your life."

Dr. Maddox looked cautiously interested.

Sennett said, "I want you to take a long, fast ride with me. And anyone who rides with me these days can very well be a gone goose. I've no less than Sheriff Damietta's confirmation of that, incidentally. We'll be headed for Lazy B, and there's many a nice spot for ambush."

"Why Lazy B?" asked Dr. Maddox warily.

"Eliot Wallace is lying out there with a Hatty bullet through his shoulder. He's in a bad way."

Apparently from nowhere, Dr. Maddox had produced a pair of saddlebags. Busily, he packed them with instruments and medicines.

Sennett said, "They'll blast me on sight, and you can be sure they won't leave you—Magistrate Maddox, the only honest man in the county—as a witness."

Making a funnel of his hands, Dr. Maddox yelled toward the kitchen. "I'm going out on a call, Cordelia. A rush call. Just wrap up some of that breakfast liver and a couple of hunks of old bread. We'll eat on the way. And come in and kiss me good-by. Be back tomorrow noon, maybe."

Sennett said, "What about those digestive juices, Doctor? What about that knife and fork and plate?"

"Digestive juices flow better when a man is in a saddle," said Dr. Maddox, rushing for the door. "Anyone should realize that."

# 14

THE FLAT, oval valley extended due north and south. At its northern end crouched the great Hatty spread, at its southern tip lay the tiny thumbprint which was Anvil; midway between them lay Napier. That was the valley's long axis: Hatty, Napier, Sennett, with many small ranches in between. Its shorter axis ran directly east and west and here, too, Napier was the hub. To the east, in the foothills, was the Durben homestead, now being tended by Dr. Maddox's nephew, Hammerhead. Up at the far north the old military road entered the valley at Hatty's, bore straight south as far as Napier, then turned west at a right angle, quartering the northwest sector of the valley like a piece of pie. Most of the northern end of the military road ran through endless Hatty land and was little traveled, except for the out-valley stageline.

The shorter spur, however, the radius which ran west from Napier, was the valley's most traveled road—and Hatty's southern boundary. In its most western reaches was Stop Six, and across the road from Stop Six, the abandoned Knutson place, where Durben and Zaragoza and Beach were now waiting. Below Knutson's began Lazy B, which, almost as interminable as Hatty's, continued south and east, in lush grazing and sleek cattle, until it eventually nudged Sennett's isolated, back-country Anvil. The Browne ranch house lay deep in its spread, miles from its nearest neighbor. Anvil's ranch house had been its closest neighbor, but a distant one.

When Sennett and Dr. Maddox left Napier, they left the town by what the doctor called its side door, by a little-used, bramble-flanked road past the slaughterhouse. Instantly out of town, they took to the open country, avoiding all trails or roads, angling their mounts south by west. They avoided, too, all signs of humanity, ranch houses, farmhouses, and homesteads, for in the last few days terror had so spread its wings that even Dr. Maddox was uncertain as to loyalties.

Early in the afternoon, they skirted a finger of land

which they knew to be Fashner property, but there was no sign of life; only copper sky, and horizon, and grass. Midafternoon they saw their first and only human, far in the distance, as they were weaving through a network of gulches, a rancher so far away he seemed scarcely three inches high. They both knew him. His name was Buddy. Dr. Maddox had brought five of his children into the world. Sennett had lent his brother money to start a herd. But now terror was on the land and loyalties were confused and shattered. Keeping carefully from his sight, they passed him by.

Just before sunset, the cloud came into the sky. The sky was amber-rose, as deep and clear as apple jelly, when it came like a flaky silver leaf above the southwestern horizon. They watched it as they rode, watched it climb, and spread and grow.

Dr. Maddox was the first to mention it. While it was still slender and flat, before it had begun to inflate and expand, he said, "That might well set us back five or six hours, if it's what it looks to be."

Sennett nodded bleakly. "If it sets us back, let's pray it sets Hatty back too."

That evening there was no twilight.

The cloud grew, bloated and ugly. Yellow vanished from the air, and high in the south and west it stretched, against a pale green stillness. Upward it churned, a rack of giant black curds blistered with olive and purple.

Then, in a golden lacework of lightning, the cloudburst came, with a howling gale. It came with a thunderclap like a blow from a gigantic mallet that smote the eardrums to deafness, and with an aftereffect that seemed to continue to pound them, with padded, soundless raps. The rain rode in then, on the wind, with force and volume that seemed to tilt the ebony world.

For what seemed like hours they fought the fury; then, gradually, the wind dropped. In time, the rain, too, ceased. The overcast cracked, split and drifted like an ice floe, and a blue, starry dome took shape above them.

They rode into the Lazy B ranch yard in the flush of a serene, fiery dawn.

Sennett had been here only once before, and again he realized it presented one of the most charming pictures he had ever seen. The ranch house was square, immaculately white, and faced on all four sides with a two-storied

115

veranda. It sat in a grove of a dozen huge trees, which were worth their weight in gold in this country, and not far from the lattice of the kitchen porch was a cool-looking, pleasant creek, crimson and satiny in the blaze of the sunrise.

There were a few shallow puddles in the ranch yard, and the creek showed a perceptible swelling. "They missed most of the bad night," said Dr. Maddox.

"What about Hatty, I wonder. He miss it, too?"

There was no one in sight. Everyone was at breakfast, probably.

Dr. Maddox dismounted, stiffly, battered and haggard, but Sennett remained in his saddle. A man appeared in the cookhouse door, wiping his mouth. It was Ed Nestor. When he saw them he yelled, and came forward at an excited lope, To Dr. Maddox, he said, "Your man's in a bedroom in the big house. He's doing all right, I guess, but he can sure use you."

With his saddlebags over his shoulder, Dr. Maddox left them.

"Light," said Nestor hospitably. "Come in and eat."

Sennett swung to the earth. "No food, thanks," he said. "I have to be moving. But I would like a fresh horse. This is a spunky little black, but she was through a baby cyclone last night."

"Do tell," said Nestor in concern. "Well, you can have the best animal on the place, and you darn well know it."

By now the entire Lazy B outfit was crowded around Sennett, top-notch punchers, bronzed and tough and leathery. There was nothing but friendship in their eyes, friendship and sympathy. They gave him almost imperceptible nods and smiles, and waited. Waited for the gory details, for him to tell them about Anvil's wrecking.

Instead, Sennett said, "Ed, go get Miss Ellen."

"She's in the big house, eating," Nestor said. "Talk to her there, and grab a piece of ham while you're at it. Don't be so stubborn."

"I want to talk to her here," said Sennett. "Right here with her men."

A wave of keen attention came from the little group of punchers.

Nestor said slowly, "I ain't sure I'm going to like this. For one thing, I don't care for anybody giving Miss Ellen orders. But I'll carry your message."

He turned on his heel and walked away.

116

A seamy-faced old cowhand named Sweetwater, who had led away Sennett's mare, now returned with a fine dappled gray. As he handed Sennett the reins, he said lazily, "I like the cut of you, Mr. Sennett. Whatever this is, I choose up with you."

"Maybe you do, and maybe you don't," Sennett said. "Why not wait and see."

Ellen came out of the house and down from the porch, walking a little behind an angry Nestor, and joined them.

She was very beautiful, startlingly attractive in the soft touch of the early sunlight, and her shoulders were very straight.

Without prelude, as though she were continuing an unspoken argument, she said, "Of course it wasn't Mr. Hatty. If you've come to accuse him I refuse to listen, and refuse to permit my men to listen. If you've come here to unsettle my men, you're not welcome. If you've come here for any other reason at all, you're more than welcome. I've known Mr. Hatty all my life, though I've never known him well until recently. He comes from one of the county's finest and oldest families. He's become a convenient whipping-boy."

Sennett raised an eyebrow quizzically. "Whipping-boy?"

"Yes. That's exactly the situation. Blame any atrocity on Mr. Hatty, that's the thing to do nowadays. Well, I'll not have him maligned, not by anyone, not in my own ranch yard."

"I haven't maligned him yet," said Sennett calmly. "But I'm just getting ready to. As you certainly must know, it was Hatty that raided Anvil."

"I know nothing of the kind. Your feud was with Holly Fashner. Now that Holly's dead, his friends must be carrying the grudge. It must have been Fashner men that wrecked Anvil."

"Fashner men were there, all right," said Sennett. "Along with Hatty men."

A murmur went through the crowd of punchers. Nestor said unbelievingly, "You must be wrong."

"What is this?" said Sennett harshly. "Do you mean you hadn't heard." Turning to Ellen, he said, "Didn't Wallace tell you?"

Ellen said, "He said something along that line. But he was rambling and mumbling and out of his head. You certainly couldn't call it reliable information."

"So you kept it to yourself."

117

"I considered that the best thing to do," she said coldly.

"He doubtless told you too that McCrae was murdered. Did you believe that?"

"Yes."

"And passed it on?"

"To my men here, yes. McCrae was loved by all of us."

"So you believed just what you wanted to, and passed on just what you wanted to."

She looked uncertain. "I tried to use my best judgment."

Now Sennett's audience was as taut as a bowstring.

He said, "What did Willie Durben say?"

"Durben didn't say anything," said Sweetwater. "He was so mad he could scarcely talk at all."

"This Hatty-Fashner business is new to all of us," said Nestor. "If it's true."

"If it's true. If it's true," said Sennett, his stubbled face creased with disgust. "Beach saw Todd Hatty. Zaragoza saw Old Man Hatty, and others, including some of the old Fashner crowd. Wallace saw Hatty's chief killer, Curley. I've just come from Napier, from a talk with King Damietta. I scared him out of his wits, and he began admitting things. You people are caught between red-hot pincers and haven't the sense to see it."

All of them, all except Ellen and Nestor, shifted angrily.

"I see it," said Sweetwater. "I been seeing it all along. I never did favor that murdering Hatty and his son."

"Miss Ellen," Sennett said formally. "I want to borrow your men, those that choose to join me. I've arranged a little meeting with Hatty, and I'd like them to stand along beside me."

"No," said Ellen, her face bloodless with rage. "And I must ask you to leave Lazy B at once. I will not permit you to come here and involve us in your lawless troubles."

Sennett ignored her. Since his arrival he had had every opportunity to give her the information he had picked up at Buttonville on her father's death, but he had refrained, considering it a cruel and improper time. Now he took a cigar from his pocket, but it was wet and sticky and he cast it from him.

Sweetwater went to the corral, saddled his horse, and returned. "As soon as I get my carbine from the bunkhouse, I'm ready to mosey," he said.

"Sweetwater, you're fired," said Nestor softly.

"Well, you're the foreman, Ed," he said. "You should

know." He ambled to the bunkhouse, returned with his rifle, and put it in its boot. To Sennett, he said, "I guess we're still going through with this, ain't we? Alone?"

"Certainly I'm going through with it," Sennett said evenly, and everyone within the sound of his voice knew that he meant it. "But we're not alone, Sweetwater. We've Beach and Zaragoza and Willie Durben with us."

"Well, that's an enjoyable surprise," said Sweetwater. "I wouldn't trade any one of them for all these hound-dogs standing around us."

"You can't go against Hatty with five men," said Nestor hoarsely.

"Can't we?" said Sweetwater amiably. "You just find yourself a nice cave and wait and see."

Sennett and Sweetwater mounted. A puncher named Lattimore got his horse from the corral, his saddle from the rail, and said, "Lattimore, you're fired. Let's go."

That started it. Singly, and in small groups, they followed suit.

Sennett wheeled, and rode, the others at a gallop beside him, and that was the way they left them—Ellen and Nestor alone in the yard, side by side; Nestor purple-red at the wattles, Ellen erect and frozen.

That was the way they left them, but hardly had they topped the first grassy rise when Nestor, his horse's hoofs flaying the ground behind them, caught up and joined them.

"These are my boys," he screamed at Sennett through the spiraling dust plumes. "I'm going along to keep them out of trouble."

They all laughed, including Sennett—and Nestor.

Well out of sight of the ranch house, Sennett slowed them with a lifted hand, and drew them into a circle about him.

Darkly flushed, he told them of his trip to Buttonville and of his interview with Buck Needham—of how Sawyer Browne had been shot down, not fairly but from ambush, and not by Needham but by Todd Hatty.

Their faces were strained and relentless as he talked.

"So that's it," Nestor said. "The Hattys have been our hidden enemies from the beginning."

Sweetwater said, "Once there was three of us—Sawyer Browne, Jim Trego, and me. When we come to Cheyenne County there wasn't no county, just Cheyennes. In our day we shared many a blanket, and many a drink, and many a rattlesnake stew. Now who's left? Just stinkin' old Sweetwater, the measliest of the lot. Where did the others go? Hatty took 'em. The more I study on this Hatty, the less I cherish him."

"It's nice to hear you talkin' about yourself, Sweetwater," Nestor said. "But you ain't exactly the point. The point is, we're wasting time."

Suddenly, as Sennett looked about him, at their drawn faces and merciless agate eyes, he felt a surge of alarm. He had expected the story to put them wholeheartedly on his side, but he had not expected, had not even considered, such a violent, boiling reaction. They concealed it well, but it was there. He wondered now if he had told them too much, if he were going to be able to keep them under control.

"We go to the Knutson place," he said. "I'll give you details later."

As they stirred to break the circle and move, young Lattimore said, "Sweetwater, I want to ask you a question. About something you know about, and I don't, but I might want to learn. How does a fellow take a scalp? Does he need a special knife? All I got is an old fifteen-cent Barlow jackknife."

"That would do fine," said Sweetwater.

They were joking, but it made pretty grisly listening.

They rode almost directly north, pushing their horses, but not overlaboring them. They would be deep in Lazy B land until they reached the Knutson boundary, so there was no need to sacrifice time for concealment. Sennett and Nestor rode in the fore, and the others followed unquestioningly. No one seemed to doubt that Sennett had the situation, whatever it might be, well in hand.

Sennett himself wondered, but felt no great uncertainty. With his arithmetical mind, he had worked out a careful schedule for Hatty. Chitwood would get word to Hatty in town, or to a Hatty rider, and the word would be carried to the far end of the valley, to the Hatty ranch house. Arrangements would certainly be made at the Hatty ranch house, for his would be no slap-dash assault; Hatty must deliver an unequivocal death blow, and he would realize it. As long as Sennett lived and appeared interested in Buttonville and Buck Needham, he would imperil all that Hatty had built up.

From Hatty's point of view, there must be no slip-up. He would strike the Knutson place with a medium band, Sennett had decided, but most importantly—to Sennett—it would be a select band, a band of Hatty's most expert killers, carefully chosen. This was important to Sennett, because these men could only be got together at the Hatty ranch. The attack, therefore, must certainly set out from the northern tip of the valley, from the Hatty ranch house.

These were the elements of Sennett's time equation: time and distance. The Hatty maneuver, having its source in Chitwood, would go north from Napier, be arranged at Hatty's, come southwest again, half the valley's length, to the Knutson place. Against that was Sennett's route: to Lazy B, and slightly north to Knutson's.

All things considered, even the variant of last night's storm gave Sennett an edge. If the storm had impeded Hatty, a good edge; if not, still an edge.

The hour of Hatty's striking, was a matter of chance. It was Sennett's guess that he would hit at night, in the dark—as he had hit Anvil.

# 15

ABOUT two in the afternoon, Sennett and his horsemen cut Knutson fence, repairing it behind them, and about four they first sighted the Knutson buildings.

Since Hatty had slain its owner, this land had stood tenantless, vacant. After Knutson's death, his cattle and horses went on the auction block, sold to Hatty. Ranch and buildings lay empty and desolate. It was good land, and many would like it, but all possible buyers held off from fear. It was well known that, when the price had dropped absurdly low, Hatty would buy it himself. It was especially important to Hatty, for it would be his first true encroachment south, past the east-west military road. He knew he had it in his pocket, so he bided his time.

The buildings lay in a sunken bowl, and when a visitor approached, he saw at first only the rolling grass broken by a windmill's wheel and the ridge of a barn. This was as Sennett and his companions saw it now.

Twenty minutes later, they were on the bowl's rim, and descending. Below them, in the hollow, were the ranch buildings, originally built about a spring. On all sides of the buildings, a short distance away, rose concave slopes of channeled, crusty clay, topped with a fringe of seared grass from the range above and beyond. The buildings were frugal except for the house, for Knutson had been a thrifty bachelor. There were two barns, cheaply painted. Behind them and beyond the springhouse, was the blacksmith shop, adjoined by a wagonshed of unpeeled poles roofed with sod. To the left of the house was Knutson's outside cellar, upthrusting from the ground perhaps three feet and with a rusty, corrugated roof. The house was in the center and the whole effect was of a loose clutter of structures, from henhouse to corncrib, without orderly pattern.

It could be a calamitous place for an ambush, and that was why Sennett had chosen it.

A crude wagon road had been cut down from the east rim to the lower level, and was the bowl's only entrance. This was the route by which Hatty would arrive.

Sennett and his companions descended the road, coming upon the house. It was, surprisingly, a two-story house. Once it had been glossy in white paint and green shutters; now it had an atmosphere of neglect.

He pulled up with his horsemen at the house steps, the Lazy B men watching him alertly, waiting for instructions. Beach, Durben, and Zaragoza came from the front door onto the porch, their rifles held loosely across their forearms. They looked ragged and mean.

Sweetwater called out to Beach. "Hallelujah, Tommy my boy. You fellows can throw away your Winchesters now and go back to bed. Lazy B has came!"

"I didn't invite you," Beach said. "But I'll try to put up with you."

To his Anvil men, Sennett said, "You wait here." To the others, he said, "Follow me."

The road which came down from the rim passed first through the scattering of sheds and barns, then looped through the front yard, passing the porch, swerving once more and terminating at the wagonshed by the blacksmith shop. Knutson, sitting on his porch, would have had this vista: dead ahead would have been the yard, then the length of road between the barns, sloping beyond and upward to the rim; to his left, at the edge of the yard and

122

about twenty yards away, the outside cellar; to his right, from the porch, open land extended perhaps a hundred yards to a brushy V-shaped split in the southern wall.

This split, Sennett knew, was a gulch mouth which led inward, bulged, finally forking off in tiny fingers of draws and ravines.

Sennett led the Lazy B riders to the gulch mouth, then paused before they entered. "Take a final look at the lay of the land," he said, quartering the bowl with his hand. "Hatty will come in at the east and head for the house in the center. You'll come at him from the south, here, and slap him from the side. I'll be with Beach and the boys at the house, throwing him off balance. You come out of this draw, full speed, as soon as you hear the first shot. He'll be in a crossfire. That's all there is to it, and if we work this right there shouldn't be any more hell in Cheyenne County. Got it?"

"Yes, we got it," said Nestor slowly. "And it looks pretty good."

Moving before them, Sennett led them into the draw. Shortly it turned, and they found themselves in a cuplike cavity rent on all sides by smaller ravines. "And here'll be a good place to wait," said Sennett. "He'll come, but I can't guarantee when. Any final questions?"

"No," said Nestor. "Just stay alive until we get there."

Suddenly the Lazy B men were in small knots, arguing and fussing.

Sweetwater said, "Mr. Sennett, what if he don't come?"

"He'll come," said Sennett.

Young Lattimore said, "We're doing this all wrong."

Some of the punchers agreed, some disagreed.

"If I was doin' it," said Sweetwater, "I'd head straight for his ranch, and I mean now. And I'd take along some dynamite. I don't hold with standing around waitin' and hopin' "

There were grunts of approval.

Lattimore said, "I sure as hell never knowed you was going to stick me back in a gulch, Mr. Sennett. I sure as hell never knowed that. I've been putting on my thinkin' cap and I've come up with a damn slick answer."

"What is it?" asked Sennett politely.

"Napier. We should ride into Napier and bust up the Pastime Saloon. Hatty owns an interest in it. It would be like spittin' in his face."

"If you followed my plan and went to his ranch house,"

said Sweetwater triumphantly, "you could spit in his face for real! By golly, I got you there, Lattimore."

"They ride well, and rope well," said Nestor defensively. "So that's why I pay 'em forty dollars a month. They ain't supposed to be geniuses."

"Can you deliver them?" said Sennett. "That's the point. When Hatty comes, and I need them, can you deliver them?"

"Of course I can't deliver them," said Nestor. "Not these boys. Nobody can deliver them. They're born and bred independent. But if I can just keep them pacified until they hear pistols goin' off, nothing can hold them."

"I see," said Sennett uneasily.

He inclined his head, raised his hand in farewell, and left them. He was a little worried as he emerged from the draw.

Beach, Zaragoza, and Durben were waiting for him on the hard earth by the front steps. He brought them up to date, telling them quickly about his conversation with Chitwood, about Damietta, about the incident at Lazy B, explaining his strategy. While Sennett talked, they listened grimly, wordlessly. They put his horse in the barn with the other three.

Then Sennett stationed them with great care, and with detailed instructions. Beach and Zaragoza he placed in each barn, across the road from each other, and said that there was to be no firing until Hatty's entire raiding party had swept past, so that their volleys would be from the rear. Durben, whom he believed to be the best marksman of the lot, he placed in the outside cellar, covering the broad flat sweep of the road before the porch. Durben was to hold his fire longest of all, until Beach and Zaragoza closed the trap, until Sennett himself had joined in.

Crouching, Durben crawled through the low door, into the cellar. Out of sight, but audible, he said, "I hate to bother you with this, but I'm curious. Are we going to be able to count on them Lazy B folks?"

Sennett started to speak, stopped, finally said, "Does it make any difference?"

"Not a bit," Durben said affably. "Fact is, I'd just as soon not have 'em clutterin' up my line of fire."

Sennett placed himself in the house, in the parlor. The house would be the focus of the attack.

Upon entering the parlor, Sennett had built a small fire in the fireplace, found an old rag rug, and put it to smouldering. A skein of smoke from the chimney would hang high in the air, he knew. Just something to raise Hatty spirits, to bring them directly to the house itself.

The little parlor was bare and musty, already giving off an unused, moldy odor. Two curtainless windows, encrusted with the grime of many rain lashings, overlooked the porch, and now Sennett took his stand by the most southern of these.

In front, the wagon road edged the porch, but dead ahead, across the sparse, dry grass of the eroded ranch yard, it looped into sight again, heading east, straight and rutted, passing between and beyond the barns, beginning its climb to the upper level. At the moment, somewhere in that upper world, the sun was setting. There was a saffron interval when the sunken world glowed dully, when long shadows stretched out from posts and sheds, and then the glow was gone, leaving only an unnatural twilight, a watery, colorless stain. There was no movement of air, nor sound.

They came within that moment of half-light. As the first blotting shadows of night, like vague purple fists, were groping outward from the encircling walls, they launched themselves down the slope; twenty riders, with a thunder of hoofs, single file, at full gallop, iron horseshoes and fetlocks bruising the baked earth of the road to billowing dust.

They were picked men, obviously. Some were known to Sennett, some were feverish, eager strangers. Curley was among them. Old Man Hatty, himself, was in the lead.

Automatically, when the first black horseman had silhouetted himself against the scarlet sky, Sennett had glanced at his watch. It said nine minutes of eight.

Down the slope in a rush they came, pounding along the road between the barns, into the ranch yard, deploying about the house, flinging themselves from their saddles. This was the instant that Sennett had set for action, and from the barns, blazing at precisely the right moment, came the guns of Beach and Zaragoza. Two men went down under their fire, one knocked over in the act of running toward the house, the other slammed from his saddle. Again and again came the venomous twin rifles of Beach and Zaragoza; a third Hatty man went down with a splintered knee, and a fourth stood foolishly with a broken arm. Somewhere along the line, Durben, from his cellar, had joined in the murderous crossfire.

In the flick of that sequence of seconds, the yard became a howling, rattling bedlam. The yells that rang out carried confusion and alarm. Some of the raiders were still mounted, some on the ground and running aimlessly, some still in the act of swinging from their stirrups. Shots seemed to be coming at them from everywhere. They knew they were trapped, but were unable to judge the strength of their oposition. Muddled, frantic, they wavered, blundered into each other, This was the period of indecesion Sennett had built his hopes on. This was the instant for Lazy B to attack.

But no Lazy B appeared.

Sennett, standing within his window, slipped, and realized he had stepped on one of his empty cartridge cases. This came as a surprise to him, for he hadn't been aware of firing. He had broken the pane before him for unhampered shooting, and this, too, had been done unconsciously. Sweat ran along his wrists, between his fingers, oozing in the palm that held his gun stock.

Outside, a new picture was taking place. Curley was reorganizing and stablizing the Hatty forces. Like a madman, he was kicking, pulling, shrieking and waving. He was pointing, too, to the barns, the cellar, the house. Men were following his advice, forming small orderly parties, concentrating their fire on the targets he indicated.

The tide was turning. With that one man, Curley, a madman in batwing chaps, the potential of the battle was being completely reversed. Durben had been snug in the little fortress of the cellar; now he was caught there, trapped, waiting only for extinction. The same was true of Sennett, in the house, and Beach and Zaragoza in the barns. Already, as Sennett watched, men appeared with armsful of dessicated shingles ripped from the blacksmith shop. It was to be fire again.

And still no Lazy B.

Well, they were digging their own graves. Had they come two minutes earlier, they would have caught the Hatty men confused, at their mercy. Wait three minutes more, and they would be up against a well organized, expert killing machine, outweighing them both in number and experience.

All through the turmoil, Old Man Hatty had sat his mount in the middle of the yard, unhit, cold and malevolent. Now he bent sidewise in his saddle and handed a passing man a jumble of tiny objects which the man caught in cupped fingers. Kitchen matches. Old Man Hatty was finally taking charge.

This thing had to be stopped, if only for a moment— had to be thrown once more into confusion. This smooth machinery must be halted, if only temporarily. Carrying his Winchester, Sennett walked from the parlor, along the hall, and out onto the porch. He opened his mouth to shout, but there was no need. Everyone seemed to see him at once.

Hell broke loose around him. A hail of wild shots sparkled at him from the yard. The rifle was slapped from his hand by flying lead, and the porch pillars on either side of his shoulders became pocked with little wisps of toothpick-sized splinters.

The greatest howl of all came from Old Man Hatty. Old Man Hatty had been among the first to see him.

He had responded in insensate fury. Raking his horse's flanks with his spurs, he came across the yard at a charge. The old man was fifty yards away when he started, and Sennett had never seen anything like it. The old man rode like a crazed Apache, and his mount seemed in full speed from the first hoofbeat.

To his right, Willie Durben came out of his cellar. An early moon hung low in the sky, and in the blue and silver of its light Durben seemed a pitifully slight figure, a small slim bundle of shabby workclothes. As steadily and deliberately as though he were threading a needle, holding his pistol in both hands, chin high and out, lining it up with rocklike precision, Willie Durben shot Old Man Hatty out of his saddle.

It was as though the old man had been caught by an invisible lariat, flung from his frothing horse, and rolled lifeless across the earth. His spurs caught in the ground as he spun, winding one leg about the other, and his mouth fell open abnormally, as though a cotterpin had been removed from his jaw hinge.

A moment of paralysis followed, then there was a flash of action down the road, by the barns.

Curley, half squatting, half prone, between the legs of a dead horse, using its body as protection, was preparing a torch. He had whittled a bundle of shingle splinters, had tied them with a length of wire, and was about to toss it on the roof of Zaragoza's barn when Hatty fell.

In the interval of shock, he had crooked his head around and stared at Hatty and the house and Sennett. Now he returned his gaze to the barns.

A figure, belly-crawling across the earth toward him, rose up in the gloom and shot him.

That was how Curley died. Tom Beach shot him with a 50-caliber carbine at eleven feet. Squarely, as it was later discovered, through the crown of the head, down through the flesh of the throat, and into the chest.

"For McCrae," said Beach in a whisper.

It was then that Lazy B roared in.

They came in their own fashion, out of the gulch mouth and in a fan across the yard, hurrahing their horses, their pistols in the air, as though it were a month-end skylark. They struck the Hatty men on their flank, and five went down under the first Lazy B fusillade. It was a wonderful and awesome thing to behold. Sweetwater, becoming suddenly and belatedly enraged, was yelling complicated curses. Nestor rode alone, and worked his deadly havoc alone. Lattimore was having the time of his life; as good a time almost, Sennett decided, as if he were busting up a saloon.

Leaderless now, the Hatty men wavered. Professional killers, they knew their job but they were befogged by confusion. And from their unprotected flank, as they wavered, they were being torn to shreds. Panic seized them. They ran helter skelter, grabbing for uninjured horses.

Only a few survived, galloping up the slope and over the rim.

With trembling hands, Sennett lighted a cigar. In the match light, he looked at his big silver watch. The entire action, he saw unbelievingly, had taken only nine minutes.

# 16

ORDINARILY, it was a four-hour ride from the Knutson place to Napier.

Sennett, Beach, Durben, and Zaragoza made it in a punishing two and a half. Leaving the shambles and its aftermath in the capable hands of Nestor, they rode hard and fast. There was only one thing left in Sennett's mind: Todd Hatty.

They were incredibly weary—even wiry little Durben reeled occasionally in his saddle—but they all knew that the job was only partly done. Certain things must be taken care of, and the most important of these was Todd Hatty.

Tying their horses at the rail before the courthouse, they walked down Main Street, toward the Pastime.

Though the hour was late for Napier, Main Street was astir. Everywhere were small groups of citizens, respectable townsmen who should have been in bed since nine, and ranchers. Shops and offices showed lights in their windows. This looked mighty like the nucleus of some vigilante business, but Sennett was certain that no news of the Knutson battle could have beaten him into town.

To Sennett's amazement, just about everyone spoke to him—and in a friendly, intimate way. No one really chatted with him, though, and for this he was glad. He was in no mood at the moment for idle conversation.

"Do you know something?" said Beach from the corner of his mouth. "I don't much like these people tonight. They got that happy bloodhound look. What they set on?"

"Nothing that concerns us," Sennett said. "Or they would have told us."

Zaragoza said, "Just the same, I wish I was back in my nice safe barn."

Todd Hatty was not in the Pastime Saloon, where Durben, despite the arguments and entreaties of the others, dropped off to wait for him. He was not in the billiard parlor either, nor in any of the central hitching lots, nor in any of the Main Street offices or shops.

"Maybe he's visiting at Popskull," said Zaragoza.

"I doubt it," said Beach. "Them Popskull gentlemen don't care for him."

On the bare earth between the Maddox house and the blacksmith shop, many men were gathered. The door had been taken from the shop and set up on whisky butts, making a big table. On this table were two lanterns, an inkpot, pens, and a huge red ledger.

Dr. Maddox, hatless and occupied, was sitting judicially on a kitchen chair, listening to murmured conversations. At times he nodded his head in agreement, or shook it angrily. A procession of men passed before the ledger, one by one, enscribing signatures; some wrote reluctantly, some fiercely, with an incensed, spluttering of the penpoint. As Sennett and his Anvil men came down the walk, silence fell over the group, and Dr. Maddox arose, advanced upon them, and blocked their way.

"Good evening, John," he said. "We were just discussing you."

Sennett tightened his lips and raised an eyebrow.

Beach said conversationally to Zaragoza, "A bunch of fellows just like this discussed a friend of mine once down at Laredo, and it broke his neck."

"The whole county's seething over Anvil, over the way Hatty wrecked it," said Dr. Maddox. "We've been expressing our sympathy for you."

"Oh," said Sennett. "Well, thank you."

They hadn't yet heard about the fight at Knutson's. It was the disaster at Anvil that had their dander up. How many days ago had that happened?

Sennett pointed to the ledger. "What's all the writing in the book?"

"That's a petition," Dr. Maddox said. "We're sending it to the Governor of the Territory, asking for his help, asking him to intervene here. This thing can't continue, and we're at our wits ends."

Sennett looked annoyed.

"In the meantime, until we can get in some outside help," said Dr. Maddox, "we intend to handle matters ourselves. We were discussing you with that in mind. We want a man to head us for law and order. We won't expect you to clean things up, of course. We just want you to try to keep things in check until assistance arrives. Will you accept?"

"Yes," said Sennett. "Gladly. On one condition."

Then, before they could answer, he told them about the battle at Knutson's.

"Smashed, completely smashed," he concluded. "I don't think there's much doubt about that."

It was a pleasure to watch their faces. Strong, honest faces, crumpled for an instant under the shock of liberation. It had all gone from them, they were telling themselves. Massacre, assassination, ambush. The coughing terror of shotgun slugs through a bedroom window, the terror of knife slashings in a dark lot, the horror of trace-chain whippings beneath a hot sun in some lonesome arroyo.

"Well," said Dr. Maddox. "You're a surprising man, John Sennett."

"He sure surprised Old Man Hatty," said Zaragoza.

"And me," said Beach.

"I surprised myself," said Sennett.

"Now," said Dr. Maddox casually, "there's nothing left but odds and ends."

"Just odds and ends," said Sennett.

The faces in the lantern light were carefully impassive. All eyes met Sennett's, and they all spoke the same silent words.

A hard-bitten rancher with buck teeth said, "Guess who I saw go in the Napier House about an hour ago?"

"Who?" asked Beach.

"That noble, snivelin', big-hearted bastard knowed far and wide to his adorin' public as Todd Emmet Hatty."

Sennett turned to leave. Dr. Maddox said, "Just one question, John."

"Yes?" said Sennett.

"You laid a condition on us. What was that condition?"

Through his thin lips, Sennett said, "That you grow up. That you never again write a petition to a governor, or to anyone else, when a third-rate chicken thief breaks into your henhouse. That you all go home, and sleep over your disgrace, and realize where that disgrace lies. With you very people yourselves, and with nobody else."

"Condition justified, and accepted," snapped Dr. Maddox.

The lobby of the Napier House, like the rest of Main Street, was brightly lighted when Sennett, Beach, and Zaragoza entered it. There were a few ranchers and townsmen here too, perhaps half a dozen. Suddenly, for the first time in days, Sennett was conscious of his soiled, battered appearance. He was proud of his immaculate, lye-scrubbed room and momentarily felt himself in grubby contrast to it.

All voices near the street door died as he entered. Beach and Zaragoza, spread on either side, slumped along slightly behind him. They looked a little bored, but businesslike, as though they were about to inventory a pen of cattle.

At the far wall of the room, just left of the closed door to the stageline office, Ellen Browne sat on an ornate sofa, a big bull's-eye mirror hanging above her head. She was dressed in soft turquoise and her golden hair was like liquid marble. Before her was a round table with a claw-and-ball pedestal and she was leaning forward, talking to the man across its surface. The mirror above her was tilted from the wall and as Sennett approached with his companions he could see the girl's face from a three-quarter front and, in the mirror, the delicacy of the back of her head and neck. Abruptly, unaccountably, she seemed intolerably desirable and necessary to him. The man across the tabletop from her was Todd Hatty.

Todd, as on the night of Dove's garden party, was rigged out in high style in his lawyer-black suit and gates-ajar collar with its faintly mildewed string tie. Much of this Sennett could judge from the back, as he advanced. He could see, too, the big animal lump of flesh bulging from the base of Todd's skull over his collar rim, about the color, and almost the size, of a beef heart. Todd, like Ellen, leaned forward as he talked and under the table Sennett could see his knee, and above the knee about three inches of rawhide. This pleased Sennett. It meant that Todd was wearing a gun. Wearing it low, for a fast draw, and thonged.

But he showed no signs of uneasiness or caution; he looked superciliously complacent.

He believes himself now the true heir apparent to Cheyenne County, Sennett decided. He has no doubt that everything has gone according to schedule. I am dead at Knutson's ranch, and only happy days lie ahead.

"All right, Todd," Sennett said wearily. "Get up."

Todd arose, slowly, as if he were hypnotized. He kept his hands away from his waist, accidentally so for Ellen's eyes, deliberately so for Sennett's. The color went out of his cheeks and throat as though it had been drained by field tile.

"Why, hello, John," he said. "You shouldn't pussyfoot up on a fellow that way behind his back. Somebody might get hurt."

He managed to make his voice joking, and at the same time overbearing and threatening.

Exhaustion swept through Sennett in a wave, and his nostrils felt dry. With effort, he said, "Todd, law and order are coming to Napier. So you and I will have to get this over in a hurry. I want you to step out in the alley with me. I'm afraid you can't bluff your way out of this."

132

Ellen said, "John! Have you gone out of your mind?"

There was slaver on Todd-Hatty's chin now and his eyes, though blank and shallow with fear, were yet sly and devious. "I've no quarrel with Anvil," he said.

"Let's walk," said Sennett.

Out burst the words that Sennett had been expecting. "Where's my old man?" asked Todd.

No one answered him.

He understands, Sennett thought. He understands and feels no sorrow. His only concern is his own survival.

Now Todd's eyes were roving, to Sennett, to Beach, back to Sennett.

He's cornered and he knows it, thought Sennett. He sees it's a showdown and he's trying to pick the softest spot. He's afraid of me, possibly because I shot Johnny Flint. Beach is an unknown quantity to him. He's considering Beach.

But it was Zaragoza whom Todd selected. Zaragoza, glum, clumsy-looking, grandfatherly. Zaragoza who stood well to one side, scarcely attentive, his hat in his gunhand.

Todd said defiantly, "If you want it, you can have it. But by the rules, right here and not in no alley where you can all take a crack at me. Right here, with Miss Ellen as a witness. But like I said, not you, John, or Beach. I got a high respeck and fondness for both of you, and I won't be driven to nothing I'll be ashamed of later. It's Zaragoza I pick. *Make it, Zaragoza!*" As Todd spoke, he pivoted heavily, and started a bumbling paw toward his holster.

Zaragoza favored a cross-draw, and his Colt was on his left hip, butt forward. His right hand, his working hand, held the hat. In a single, flashing movement, he slapped the hat on his head, askew, threw his hand continuously around and down—and made his draw. Todd's .45 had hardly left its leather when he caught three slamming bullets in his heart. He went down like a bale of hay.

In the pulsating vacuum that followed, Beach said accusingly, "You done that whole thing on purpose, Hilario. You baited him in from the beginning, holding your hat in your gunhand and all, on purpose. You could have at least dropped the hat, instead of putting it on that knucklehead of yours."

"Drop my dirty old hat on John's nice clean lobby floor?" said Zaragoza.

Sennett said roughly, "Listen to me, Hilario. Never do that again. Do you understand?"

"Yes sir," said Zaragoza cheerfully.

Lew Julián, the hotel manager, joined them, grinning delightedly. Finally, when Ellen was able to speak, she said, "That was the most brutal thing I ever saw."

"The trouble is," said Sennett, "you've been missing these brutal things. Actually, this is a weak sample. Much worse things have been happening, and you well know it, but because you don't see them with your own eyes, and because it's pleasant to live in a dream world, you refuse to let them agitate you." He paused. "Please excuse me, Ellen. I don't know what I'm saying. What I've just said isn't true at all. Things have been cracking open so fast that I guess I'm a little off balance."

She stared at him wordlessly, pale and shaken.

He said gently, "What are you doing in town, anyway?"

"I came in with Dr. Maddox. I was worried about you."

He pretended not to hear. "Can you take a blow?" he asked. "A real blow?"

She hesitated, and nodded.

"Good," he said quietly. "I'd advise it. It'll get you out of that hell you've been living in. Come along with us. I want to talk with Chitwood, and I want to talk with Damietta." To Beach and Zaragoza, he said, "All right, boys. We'll be on our way."

They left the hotel and went out onto the sidewalk, Ellen and Sennett in the lead, Beach and Zaragoza following closely. The town's excitement was growing, rather than decreasing; lanterns on chairs and stools had now appeared by store fronts and now, too, there were more ranchers, drawn in from their homes.

As Sennett and his friends neared the barbershop, a wild man burst through the throng. It was Hal Durben, half dressed, reeling and staggering. In his hand he had an old Sharps buffalo gun, a twenty-pounder, one of those monstrosities that could blast out with a two-inch, two-ounce slug of lead. Frantically, he yelled, "Am I in time?"

Sennett took his arm, and led him to one side. "What are you doing out of bed?"

"Am I in time?"

"Where in heaven's name did you get that gun?"

"Mrs. Maddox loaned it to me. Am I in time? Where's Old Man Hatty?"

"Late and lamented," said Sennett.

When Hal opened his mouth to complain, Sennett said, "Also Curley, your friend. And also Todd. Willie's in the Pastime, no doubt conscientiously refraining from bourbon. There's no need for that any more. Why don't you join him and tell him it's about all over, that he can celebrate."

"Well, I'm in time for that, anyway," Hal said jubilantly.

Staggering and reeling, he was on his way.

Sennett rejoined the others. They made their way to Stable Street.

The stable, deep in the shadows, loomed dark and indistinct. Walking down the passage by its side, Sennett and his friends came into the yard at the rear. Overhead, the stars were low and bright in the lavender sky. To their left, at the edge of the yard, midway in the row of sheds that flanked it, was the rebuilt and refurbished shed which Chitwood used as a home. A pencil of light came from beneath its doorsill.

Too many things are happening in town tonight, Sennett thought. He can't sleep. They crossed the yard, and Sennett knocked on the door.

Inside, after a moment, there was a bumping around, and the door came open about three inches. Sennett said, "Dewey, it's finished. I haven't time to go into details, but you'd better take my word for it. There's no more Hatty. What about you? How shall it be?"

Through the doorway, desperately, Chitwood said, "You people out there hold steady now. Hold steady. Remember Dr. Maddox. Dr. Maddox stands for law and order."

"I've Beach with me," Sennett said quietly. "And Zaragoza. Make up your mind."

They could hear Chitwood breathing thickly, frightened. "I've made up my mind," he said at last. "I'm coming out. With my hands up. I'm throwing myself on your mercy."

He emerged into the moonlight.

"I've been to Buttonville, Dewey," Sennett said. "I've talked to Buck Needham. I know the whole story, but I want to hear it from your lips."

Chitwood's eyes adjusted themselves to the night. Puzzled, he said, "Why, they's a woman with you." Stridently, he added, "It's Miss Ellen! My God, you brought Miss Ellen here so she could shoot me!"

"Nobody's going to shoot you, Dewey," Sennett said,

"if you unload the truth. Funny thing, but your words are worth more to us than your corpse. Talk, and you can go. That's a promise."

"It's a pretty bad story for her to listen to."

"If she doesn't hear it from you, she'll hear it from me. Talk."

"All right," said Chitwood quietly, "here it is. She should hear about it anyway. About how Sawyer Browne got killed. He wasn't drunk that night, like they said. He was as sober as Judge Maddox." In his moment of stress, Chitwood couldn't seem to get Maddox out of his mind. "He was as sober as that wonderful man, Judge Maddox, and he never really quarreled with Buck Needham."

He paused. "For a long time I'd been a Hatty man. My livery stable made a mighty fine place for them out-of-county gunnies to hide their mounts. Well, that afternoon Todd Hatty come to me and said he wanted to sit in my office and wait a while. He and his old man had it all schemed out, but I didn't know it till afterward. He said Sawyer Browne would be around a little later, for his horse, to get back to Lazy B, and when he came I was to stop him in the passage and ask him how come General Lee held Richmond so long against the Yankees. You see, the battles of the war, and strategy and all, was Sawyer's weakness. If he got started talking about it, he couldn't quit. I didn't see no real harm in this, so I did like they told me."

"This is the truth," Ellen said softly. "He's telling the truth. Father would talk to kingdom come about it."

"So I did like they told me," resumed Chitwood. "About early dusk Sawyer showed up and I stopped him and got him talkin' Todd was sitting in the office, in the twilight, just out of sight. We'd been talkin' about ten minutes or so when Buck Needham come down the passage. Sawyer was just putting a match to a cigar. Neither Buck or Sawyer ever said a word to each other. I lied when I said they quarreled. Sawyer hardly noticed Buck.

"Inside the office, Todd was standing by his window now. He called, 'Mr. Browne!' and I guess all of us turned. That was what Todd wanted, you see, to get Sawyer from the front. Todd shot Sawyer three times. Sawyer's gun was never out of its holster until later, when Todd yanked it out. Afterwards, they told me what to say at the inquest and I done it. I suppose you think I'm a pretty wicked man, Miss Ellen."

"Why, no," said Beach. "We don't none of us think that. We think you're a fine upstanding citizen who just happens to have an annoyin' weakness. We worship you."

"You're a good man," said Zaragoza gravely. "Too good to live."

Sennett said, "Go into that barn, Dewey. Pick out your best horse, and get out of the county. These boys of mine have had a bad night." Brooding a moment, he said, "My promise expires at dawn."

Ellen had nothing to say on the way back to Main Street, and they left her to her silence. This must be a very bad instant for her, the instant in which her tortured mind was readjusting itself—but the worst was over. Once, as they walked, she suddenly took Sennett's hand, and as suddenly dropped it; and that was almost excruciating to him. It was as though a white-hot spike had been driven through his heart. On Main Street, they started their search for Damietta.

Sennett considered this visit with Damietta necessary, and had taken Ellen along for a special purpose. He had planned it to follow the session with Chitwood, thinking it might distract her, might help stabilize her in this interval of shock.

Damietta was not in the jail office.

Getting information from a rancher before the barber-shop, they learned he had been seen entering the court-house.

They found him at the end of the ground-floor corridor, in the records' room. If he wasn't hiding, Sennett decided, it was the next thing to it. The room was hardly more than a cubbyhole, and without windows. It was shelved on three sides and the shelves were a jumble of calf-bound books, pasteboard boxes, and sheaves and rolls of foolscap. There was no furniture but a crude hickory chair. Sheriff King Damietta sat on this chair, hunched dejectedly forward, forearms on his knees. On the floor planking before him was a kerosene lamp. If he had looked depraved and brutish before, now he looked simply stupid and scared.

They entered, the three men and the girl, and lined up before him. His huge, blubbery hands trembled. Slowly, with great muscular effort, he tried to smile, lifting his upper lip in a grimace and revealing his grubby teeth.

"I hear there's been bad trouble out at Knutson's," he said. "And some says Zaragoza here killed Todd Hatty,

137

but in a fair fight. You come to report it, Mr. Sennett?"

"No," said Sennett.

"Then what did you want? Can't you see I'm mighty busy?"

"I want you to hold still," said Sennett. "Just hold still and don't move. Think you can do it?"

"If you say so, Mr. Sennett," he said. His eyes were glassy with terror now. "But what are you people up to? I don't get what you mean." He froze in his chair, motionless except for his hands, which quivered uncontrollably.

Sennett leaned forward and unpinned Damietta's badge. Holding it impressively, he offered it to Zaragoza.

"Oh, no you don't," said Zaragoza, recoiling. "Not to me."

"I hate to lose a foreman," said Sennett. "But how about you, Tom?"

Beach screwed up his face.

"He's thinking," Sennett explained to Ellen.

"About what?" she asked. Already she was beginning to relax.

Beach said, "I'm thinking about my past life. And tryin' to make up my mind. As near as I can recollect, I been about everything but a sheriff. By golly, yes, sir, I'll take a crack at it."

"Shake hands with the new sheriff, Mr. Damietta," said Sennett, handing Beach the badge.

Damietta was out of his chair in a bound, grabbing Beach's hand, pumping it wildly.

"Congratulations," he wheezed. "Congratulations!"

When they left the courthouse, Ellen was actually smiling. It was a small, shy smile, but it was there. Tears had dried at the corners of her eyes, tears which had come without the sound of weeping, tears which Sennett had been unaware of until now, until he saw their flecked glaze in the light from a shop window.

At the corner of Plum and Main, he said, "Here I must leave you. Will you escort Miss Ellen back to the hotel, boys? I'll see you all in the morning. There's one more thing on my agenda."

For an hour, he had been troubled over Dove, placing himself in her mind, knowing she must be rent with anxiety over him.

"I'll wait for you in the lobby," said Ellen.

"No," said Sennett firmly. "You must go to bed. I may be very late. I'll see you in the morning."

"I'm too tired to sleep," she said. "I'll wait."

She said it pleasantly, but there was a touch of granite in her voice.

They stared at her. To all of them, this was an unsuspected Ellen Browne. Sweet, and lovely, but suddenly—for no reason at all—muleheaded.

# 17

ALONE, Sennett walked down Plum Street.

The job was done, the snake nest utterly destroyed. Now, for the first time, perhaps, Cheyenne County could live a normal and decent life. Its future, as Sennett realized possibly even more than the others, was golden. It had the fattest cattle in the territory, the lushest grass— and soon it would have a railroad. Now that Hatty's slave whip had disintegrated, it was on the verge of undreamed opulence. Almost overnight, almost before the gunsmoke had dissipated from Knutson's barnyard, it would become a powerful and flourishing community. It was a dreadful and strange thing how the evil in one man's soul could corrupt such abundance.

The past week had brought other unbelievable changes, too. The most important of these, from Sennett's point of view, was the community's new attitude toward him. For three years, since his arrival, he had been respected, but friendless. How greatly this had reversed itself he had learned from Dr. Maddox and his friends, and, in the past few minutes on Main Street, from many others. Respect had gone into admiration, which was quite a different thing. Everywhere he had seen in smiles, and in quiet, thoughtful eyes, true friendship.

Plum Street was asleep and the Stafford house, it seemed to him as he climbed the steps to the dark porch, was even more soundly asleep than its neighbors.

The notches between his fingers felt grimy as he knocked on the door, and a rip in his coat shoulder, caught somewhere on a nail at Knutson's, flapped up against his neck; as he attempted to smooth it back in place he could feel where the tailor's padding thrust out in knots and bunches. His hand against his cheek touched unkempt, hairy stubble; he wondered how long it had been since he had held a razor. Most of all, though, he was in a near fog from fatigue. Once more he knocked on the door, and more loudly, simultaneously clanging the bell-pull.

A faint light appeared from within, and through a slit in the lace curtain he could see Mrs. Stafford descending the stairs, a candle held high above her head. She was bundled to the chin in a thick, bulky dressing robe, and her throat wove back and forth in anger at being awakened. Her puckered, poisonous mouth seemed to be muttering complaints and epithets.

Opening the door, she said malignantly, "Oh, it's you. What do you want?"

"I'd like to speak to Dove," Sennett said.

"My baby's in bed. Like all respectable folks should be."

"And I think she'd like to speak to me, too," said Sennett mildly. "If you won't bother to bring her down, I'll simply go around to the side of the house and call her."

"And wake all the neighbors?" said Mrs. Stafford venomously. "Come in. Don't just stand there, come in."

Sennett entered the hall, and she closed the door behind him; closed it and locked it. Taking an umbrella from the stand, she rapped its handle noisily against the newel post.

Craning her neck up the stairwell, she yelled, "Aubrey, Dove. It's John Sennett. He forced his way in. It's that John Sennett."

The way she yelled, you'd think he was a stranger.

Then, to his bewilderment, she extinguished the candle. "Folks might be coming by on the sidewalk," she explained. "And I don't want them peeking in, seeing me in my robe." Her tone of voice, the fact that she explained it at all, told him that she was lying, that she was deliberately misrepresenting her action. Upstairs, now, he could hear the groggy movement of sleepers arisen.

"We'll go back to the study," she said. "Dove can talk to you there."

He groped his way behind her, along the dark hall. At the study door, she told him to wait, entered, then called him. As he stepped in, he saw that she had pulled the draperies and lighted the lamp. Now, more than ever, this room depressed him. In the sickly, smoky glow of the big china lamp, everything in it, muddy varnish, plum-and-bronze wallpaper, the heavy black furniture, seemed un-

140

wholesome, funereal. As usual, too, the airless room was stiffling with the odor of lint and Mr. Stafford's hair oil.

Speaking softly, he said, "Did you get the bolt of China silk and did you like it?"

"I got it, but I didn't like it."

"And you don't like me either, really, do you? You never have, have you?"

"In private, I'll tell you," she said. "I loathe and despise you. You come into Napier a down-at-heels stranger, and fall into a little easy money, and right away you think you're good enough for the sweetest angel this county ever produced, my baby. You've got no family, no bloodlines, nothing, and with me it's family that counts. With Mr. Stafford, of course, it's money. That was the way you got around Mr. Stafford. Money. I can't for the life of me see how you ever got around little Dove. She had the cream of the county to pick from, and she could have had any of them by crooking her finger, and it's you she dredged up."

"Well," said Sennett. "That's clear enough. And I'm in your debt. It's nice to know just how you feel about me, but to be honest, I suspected it."

Dove and her father came into the study. Dove had a delicious, frothy, little girl look, sleepy-eyed, incredibly enchanting in a cloud of pink ruffles. She gave Sennett a restrained, mischievous smile. Mr. Stafford gave Sennett no smile at all. Apparently still stupefied from slumber, he bungled across the room, striking the edge of the table, striking the corner of the sofa, and flopped into his big easy chair. In a fashion, he had managed to dress. At least he had peeled on his skin-tight pants; he wore a misbuttoned shirt, too, but without collar or cuffs.

Pompously, his face gleaming, he said, "This is a rather inconvenient hour to come visiting, John. But perhaps it's just as well. I believe Dove wants to talk with you."

"I want to talk with her, too," Sennett said goodnaturedly. "I wonder if you kind people would mind leaving the room a few minutes, so we can be alone."

"We have no secrets in this family," Mrs. Stafford said. "And it's taking you a long time to realize it."

"I want them to stay," said Dove. She touched his wrist, shielding the action slightly from her parents with her body. "John, we've had some pretty good times together, haven't we?"

A little startled, Sennett nodded. "Reasonably good."

141

"You've given me presents, I've given you presents. Give and take. No one obligated to no one. Isn't that right?"

"Yes," said Sennett. "But this is probably the strangest conversation I ever engaged in."

"And you know I have a deep affection for you?"

"Dove!" said Mrs. Stafford.

This one, Sennett didn't even bother to answer. He got out a cigar, offered it to Mr. Stafford, who refused it, and lighted it himself.

"Papa thinks you might have misunderstood all this," Dove said earnestly. "He thinks I've led you to love me."

"Papa's right," said Sennett. "In fact it's my impression that we're engaged to be married."

Arranging her face to portray extreme distress, Dove said, "But how could you have got that idea? Look. You've never even given me a ring."

"I gave you a ring."

"A ruby ring, yes. But officially we agreed it wasn't an engagement ring, didn't we?"

This was unbelievable to Sennett. Calmly, he said, "An engagement is a contract. And in a contract I like to get my facts straight. Are we engaged, or aren't we?"

"No, John," she said sorrowfully. "But there are other girls, and you're still young."

"Now you'd better leave," Mrs. Stafford said brusquely. "And by the back door."

Watching Mr. Stafford fidget, Sennett asked, "And what's wrong with you?"

"Not me, my boy," Mr. Stafford said heavily. "With you. I might as well come right out with it. You're not fooling anybody. We all know why you're here. You've harried and insulted the Hattys intolerably. Now your ranch has been destroyed. At this very minute, without a doubt, you are being hunted down by Mr. Hatty and his men. Hunted down like a rabbit. You have come to us, expecting us to aid you, possibly to hide you."

"Have you been down town tonight?" Sennett asked.

"No. There are too many lights on Main Street. Something rowdy is taking place. On such nights my family and I stay at home."

They'd heard of the wrecking of Anvil, but nothing since.

"I've really enjoyed this conversation," Sennett said politely. "It's been truly educational."

142

Stiffly, and yet at the same time exuberant, thinking of Ellen, Sennett got to his feet.

"Anyone can make a mistake, John," said Mr. Stafford pontifically. "And you'll have to admit I've told you all along that you were acting unwisely. I won't say you deserve it, but I will say you've used poor judgment."

"I have indeed," said Sennett dourly.

Mr. Stafford plumped his bulbous lips. He made great business of hooking on a pair of crescent-lensed spectacles and sat back in his chair with an air of importance.

"Things have been happening rapidly here for the past few days," he announced. "A great many changes have taken place, significant changes, and I think I might inform you that I have somewhat gained in importance. Before you came to the valley I was Napier's leading financial personage. I might even say, without immodesty, simply that I was its leading personage. Now I don't want to give you the idea for a moment that you pushed me from the limelight, but I must admit that through a series of lucky events you managed to acquire a certain amount of prestige. You know your position now. Would you be interested in hearing about mine?"

"I'm in pretty much of a hurry to get out that door," said Sennett. "But go right ahead. Tell me."

"Very well, I shall. The North and South Associations have merged—"

North and South Associations, thought Sennett. How long ago that was to him, but how recent it must be to others.

"The North and South Associations have merged under the guidance of Mr. Hatty," said Mr. Stafford. "Can you grasp that? Can you actually conceive what that means? The entire valley, with all its resources, is now under Mr. Hatty's shrewd sponsorship. Now such a tremendous organization as this must require a highly competent assistant advisor. This advisor, of course, will be its secretary-treasurer. Would you like to try to guess this man?"

"I have a feeling it's you," said Sennett.

"It is indeed. Think of it! I'm practically in charge of the whole county!"

"I'm a little tired," said Sennett. "If you'll all excuse me, I think I'll go back to my hotel and get some sleep."

No one moved, so he said, "I can find my way out alone. By the back door."

Ellen, as she had promised, was waiting for him in the

Napier House lobby. She was again sitting under the mirror by the wall. Todd Hatty's body was gone now, of course, and Julian had sponged the old rug and covered it with a piece of new carpeting, for the time being. As Sennett approached her, he was glad to see her sitting just where she was. This meant to him that she had already conquered part of the horror of the evening. With time, he knew, with gentleness and with love, she would wipe out the whole ugly picture.

He sat beside her, and took her hand, and she said, "How is Dove taking all this?"

Stunned that she even knew Dove's name—though of course she must—and embarrassed that she so intuitively understood his goings and comings, he said, "She broke her engagement with me. It turns out, according to her, that we've just been having a good time together."

Crinkles came into the corners of his eyes, and his mouth dropped open in a silent laugh at the sheer absurdity of it.

"I'm glad to see you're not bitter over it," she said seriously. "I'm glad you aren't mortally hurt."

"Well, I'm not," he said. "I'm just hungry. Let's go into the kitchen and see what we can find. That's a nice thing about owning a hotel. When you own a hotel, you own a kitchen."

"When you get married you own a kitchen, too," she said, and kissed him.

"You know, a funny thing," he said. "After that night in the sitting room here I thought I was in love with both of you. It made me feel terrible."

"That's all I want to know," she said, and laughed. "Now let me tell you something about this romance business. The new automatically cancels out and voids the old. The minute it happened, the very minute it began to worry you, Dove had lost you irretrievably. Now one thing more. Come to my ranch, and run it for me."

"No," said Sennett. "I'm building Anvil up again, from scratch. And I'll do it right this time. It'll be quite a job, though. Will you help me?"

"Yes," she said.